One Love

Book 2:

Canyon Road Love Stories

by

Thea Thomas

Books by Thea Thomas

The Canyon Road Love Stories series:
Canyon Road
One Love
Two Weddings

YA:
The People in the Mirror

Dark Urban:
Amethyst Dreams

Thea's books in both ebook and paperback
can be found wherever books are sold.

One Love

Book 2:

Canyon Road Love Stories

by

Thea Thomas

One Love

Book 2:

Canyon Road Love Stories

Contemporary Sweet Romance

Thea Thomas

Emerson & Tilman, Publishers
129 Pendleton Way #55
Washougal, WA 98671
All Rights Reserved

Book & cover design by Emerson & Tilman
Thea@EmersonandTilman.com

Copyright © Thea Thomas/Emerson & Tilman
Thank you to © Blythe Ayne for the Love Poetry
Paperback ISBN: 978-1-947151-38-3
[1. FICTION/Romance/Contemporary
2. FICTION/Contemporary Women
3. FICTION/Romance/General] I. Title
BIC: FM
First Edition

DEDICATION:

*To All Who Believe
In the Power of Love*

Chapter 1
Anthony's Birthday Party

Anthony's birthday party! The music swelled in tempo and volume as the dance floor became crowded to its limit. Alison smiled at Sage as she and Michael whirled by. How perfectly suited for one another, Alison thought, and how beautiful!

She glanced at Anthony by her side, engaged in conversation with another well-wisher. Tom, Alison believed, but she wasn't quite sure. She could not escape the feelings mounting in her of being out of place—of the intermittent awkwardness from people here, that she'd not seen in ages. People from her past, living their lives in a place far removed from her present world and life.

She needed a few moments to herself. As she slipped away, she nodded and smiled at Anthony. He gave her a side-long glance that begged her not to go. But she had to spend a few moments alone.

So much happening!

She stepped outside to drink in the brisk braced-with-autumn breeze. The incredible alabaster sheen of the moon bathed everything in sight, shadows slid out around the plants, the walkway, the white columns holding up the portico. The Pacific Ocean glowed under the bright moon with a driving energy, while its waves came gliding in, whispering and sighing, to shore.

So surreal, so dream-like. Though she'd not been here in years, that long-ago time rolled over her like the ocean waves, unstoppable, unbidden.

Shivering, she returned inside, then wandered down the hall away from the party, deep in reflection. As she passed the partially closed kitchen door, the caterers, Sage's dear friends, Tina, and John, were engaged in a conversation that tore the roof off her musings.

"I couldn't be happier to see Sage finally hooking up with Michael," Tina said. "It's about time!"

Both she and John, had their backs to the door, fussing over a dessert. He nodded, "Obvious couple. Not as obvious as you and I, my pumpkin jewel," he reached over and pinched her cheek, spreading powdered sugar everywhere.

Alison smiled at their charming, affectionate interaction.

Tina giggled. "True. Not as made-for-each-other as we are, my heart. We broke the mold. But, Lordy, am I relieved that that whole thing with Anthony went by-the-by."

Alison's smile disappeared, replaced by a wave of shock.

"That was *ridiculous,*" he agreed. "What was that old geezer thinking?"

"Wellllll...he *is* gorgeous and he *is* rich."

"True points, both, Tina. But still. Look at Sage...."

"Yes. There's only one Sage. Ya just want to hate her 'cause she's so friggin' beautiful. But then, she's so sweet, you gotta love her. Boy, I thought Anthony would pop the question tonight. I feared he might, in front of all his friends."

"Feared?"

"Yeah, because I don't think Sage would have said yes."

"You don't?"

"No.

"Why not?"

"Oh, silly boy, you know why not..."

"Because she's honest, through and through. And you and I know—even when she didn't know it herself—that she's in love with Michael. No matter how much she was mad at him...."

"Exactly, brilliant! Right on every point. And then, of course, Anthony wouldn't do such a thing in front of Alison."

"No, he wouldn't," John agreed. "Do you think maybe ... maybe Sage had that in mind when inviting her?"

"Oh!" Tina exclaimed, "I didn't think of that." She paused for a moment. "No, I seriously doubt it. Sage just wants everyone to be happy. And she adores Alison. No, she just wanted everyone who could make it to Anthony's birthday party to be here.

"All righty, this thing's ready, let's get it out to the starving masses."

Alison hurried further down the dark hall and turned a corner. She stood for several minutes to recover and reflect. *Was it at all possible that Anthony had in mind to marry Sage?* She couldn't even put thought to it. How could he? He'd been like an uncle to her, ever since she'd come to live with her Aunt Victoria as a young girl.

Was it possible? Alison's anger, which she rarely felt, rose right through her, and settled in her forehead, a dull, inescapable pain. After all she'd endured because of Victoria, and now ... *oh!* She couldn't think about it.

She breathed deeply for fully a minute, releasing the frustration and pain, and, along with it, the headache. She finally gathered herself enough to return down the hall, putting on her calm face, her strong face. She'd appear to enjoy herself. Sage deserved that.

As Alison put a closing thought—at least for the moment—on this impossible news, Anthony came hurrying down the hall toward her. "My dear," he exclaimed, "I couldn't *find you!*"

She smiled. "Oh, you know, I needed a moment alone. I stepped outside, but it was a bit chilly."

Anthony gave her a long, quizzical stare. Yes, he knew her so well. But she would not voice her thoughts ... her shocked, confused, thoughts. She'd have plenty of time to reflect on everything, once she got back to San Francisco, which she now fervently wished she'd never left.

She and Anthony reentered the party. Sage immediately made eye-contact with her. "Everything all right?" her look asked.

Alison nodded, smiling brightly. Sage, too, knew her so well. Her heart went out to Sage, who, trying to make everyone happy, still had about her the aura of sadness.

Oh, the whole thing was a complete tangle. And Alison had come to love her uncomplicated life, far from here.

She knew she'd not stay in Orange County the planned five days. She'd, spend a couple days with Sage—well, if Sage *wanted* to spend two days with her, Alison thought, taking in the eye-lock between her and Michael. The two of them had a lot of lost time to make up. Perhaps Sage would be relieved when Alison told her she intended to cut her stay short.

*　*

"**W**hat do you mean, you're going back to San Francisco day after tomorrow?" Sage protested the next morning, as they sat over cups of hot tea in Sage's rose garden, that, even at the end of the season, bathed them in the aroma of roses. They enjoyed a lazy chat as they waited for Anthony and Michael to arrive.

"I'm sorry, Sage. I have a seminar Tuesday that slipped my mind," Alison half-lied. She hadn't forgotten the seminar at all. It was online, and she'd fully intended to teach it from Sage's home.

"I got so caught up in coming down here, that I forgot about it, and my calendar just reminded me this morning that I need to pull the materials together this weekend. I can do that at the last minute, so I'll stay the weekend, but then, I must leave. Also, I have a big gallery show opening next weekend, that I really need to concentrate on."

True disappointment passed Sage's features.

"Oh, Sweetie," Alison reached out and took Sage's hand. "It's all right. We'll make it up, yes? Now that our relationship has found a new life, I can't wait to have you, and maybe Michael, too? come and visit me!"

Thea Thomas – 5

Sage brightened. "Oh, yes, Alison, I'd really, truly love to visit you. I feel the same, I don't want to lose you again. When I was a little girl," tears threatened at the corners of Sage's eyes, "when I was a little girl, there were times when I thought of you as my aunt, too. You were always so kind to me. And there were times when Aunt Victoria—as much as I loved her!—was anything but kind."

"*Ah!* Let us not think of such things," Alison exclaimed. "I'm honored to be your aunt, and I lay claim to the title here and now!"

The chimes at the back door rang out, announcing the arrival of Anthony and Michael.

"Oh, boy, breakfast." Sage laughed. "The men promised to make it, and I'm holding them to it!"

"Indeed," Alison agreed as they walked through the house to answer the door.

When Sage opened the door, the two gorgeous men entered, carrying ridiculous amounts of groceries.

"We come bearing gifts of comestibles," Anthony declared.

Sage laughed, opening the door wider. "Enter! We're starving, though I don't know why, with all we had to eat last night."

Anthony nodded. "Amazing talent, those two friends of yours."

The four of them moved through the hall and into the kitchen. "So true," Sage agreed. She gestured to the kitchen counters. "Place your offerings here, and let's see what you've brought."

They set everything down. Michael smiled almost shyly at Sage. "Missed you, last night," he whispered, giving her a hug.

"Me too, you." Sage leaned into his embrace.

Alison and Anthony stood back beaming at them, as if they'd scripted the entire scene. Anthony took a picture with an invisible camera. "Such a sight! Warms my heart. *Warms my heart!* How did we not see this, years ago, dear Alison? This beautiful and perfect, couple...." He turned to her, smiling.

"They were children. And Michael stayed with us only a total of three or four weeks, after Sage came to live with ... came to live here. When he was a bit older, he had ...."

"I had summer jobs, that's right," Michael nodded, starting to organize the food. "But had I known my future was in the neighboring castle, I would have ridden my charger over here every day!" Without another word, he fell to making a breakfast that half a dozen people couldn't eat, directing Anthony as his *sous-chef*. Finally the two men arranged everything beautifully on the dining room table, where Sage and Alison had sat, watching in rapt attention at the men's culinary skills.

"Pretty as a picture," Alison declared.

They stood admiring the picture perfect meal for a few moments. "All right, enough of that, let's eat!" Sage gestured, and everyone found their place without further dallying.

After a few minutes of indulged noshing, Sage dropped Alison's bombshell. "Alison just informed me that she's only going to stay a couple more days instead of the intended five days."

Anthony dropped his fork. "Oh! Alison, please stay. I've been so happy all morning...."

Alison glanced at Anthony, but then lowered her gaze to her plate. "I'm sorry if this actually disappoints anyone! I didn't imagine that it possibly could. But, as I told Sage, I … I have a seminar that I completely forgot about with all the short notice stirring everything up to come here. The seminar's a one-off, and fell off my radar until my calendar reminded me this morning that I had to pull the materials together.

"And I have a gallery show opening next weekend that I must concentrate on. Coming here was so spontaneous, that I rather much forgot my obligations …."

Michael, who had been silent, said softly, "I'm really sorry that you can't stay longer, Aunt Alison."

That just about did Alison in—Michael hadn't called her "Aunt Alison" since he was a boy.

She raised her gaze to make eye contact with every one of them in turn, more torn than they realized. "I'd love to, but my materials are at home, and I can't hold up blank sheets of paper as examples of my techniques." She shook her head as if disappointed, but really, she was in despair. She wouldn't hurt any of these people for anything—even including Anthony, despite all he'd hurt her in her life. But—she simply *Could. Not. Stay.*

Even now, this moment, she thought she might start to scream—which she'd *almost* never done in her life, and certainly not around anyone who could hear her.

The only way she imagined she could make it through the next two days was to be either utterly engaged in some activity, or completely alone in her room. The danger of being one-on-one with Anthony loomed like an impossible threat.

And, yes, she did—so much!—want to be with both Michael and Sage, together and individually. "But, Michael, you and Sage will come and visit me, will you not?" she asked.

Michael glanced at Sage, and she nodded enthusiastically. "Of course, dear Alison, try to keep us away."

"Yes," Sage agreed. "Try to keep us away."

"All right then. That's settled. Let's get into the here and now—what's the game plan for the weekend?"

"All dependent upon your desire, Alison," Sage said. "The art museum, riding—the horses could use some exercise, am I right, Anthony?"

"*Absolutely!*"

"Dinner at the place of your choice," Sage continued. The theatre. La Boéme is playing to rave reviews. The Fullerton Arboretum is beautiful. Tina and I took John there recently, and he loved it. Whatever else you fancy."

Alison chuckled. "I believe you've outlined a week's worth of activity."

"Oh, no, not quite. I also had the idea of going to San Diego for a day, or taking a little cruise to Catalina island ... or both."

"Lovely ideas, Sage! But I particularly like the idea of a good ride both days. Twinkle Toes is the daughter of my horse, is she not?"

"She is!" Anthony said. "She'll love you. That's a great idea, to have you and Twinkle bond. I'll take Thor and Sage ...."

"I'll be on Magenta, Thor's daughter. She's the most beautiful horse you'll ever see. That strange, reddish purple sheen to her nearly-black hide."

"She is a rare beauty," Anthony agreed, looking pointedly at Alison.

And I'll ride Magenta's mother, Scarlet," Michael added.

Alison took in Michael's contemplation of Anthony's gaze at her. Altogether a peculiar discomfort.

She glanced at Sage, who seemed pleased with herself, as if she'd master-minded a wonderful thing.

Unhappily, a wonderful thing, as it included being around Anthony, it was not.

Chapter 2
The Next Day

After a thoroughly indulged breakfast where they all complained of over-eating, they retired to the rose garden.

The tiny, shabby chic wrought iron table hardly held all their paraphernalia, but somehow, Alison thought, Sage made it come together beautifully, pulling up a wooden bench that Anthony and Michael sat on, in close double *tête-à-tête* with Sage and herself.

Sage and Michael were in heaven, Alison told herself, let this be about them. For the time being, she must set aside her own discomfort, happy observing the shy, blossoming love between the two young people whom she adored.

"What are you reflecting on, with such intensity?" Anthony asked.

"*Oh!*" Alison smiled, "You caught me!" She nodded at Sage and Michael. "I was just thinking about these two beautiful children, and how ... how sweet it is that they've found one another. How perfect. How uncomplicated."

"Not entirely uncomplicated," Sage said, pouring Michael's tea. No, we wasted entirely too much time making it complicated. Even though fate, with its large, insistent hand, tried to put us together long ago."

Michael took Sage's hand as soon as she set down the teapot. "We could have taken a straight path, from the first...."

"When that motorcycle gang forced me into the ditch with that ridiculous whale of a car I had. There you came over the hill in your little vintage MGB, and saved me."

"I don't know that I exactly *saved* you ...."

"You did! You saved me. And ... let the record show that I ... I," she looked down shyly, "I was attracted to you from the first moment I got a good look at you, when you drove me up to the house. I looked at that tousle of brown hair, and your sincere, guileless, profile in the nearly-dark car and something went *bing!* in my heart. After which I spent an inordinate amount of time trying to ignore it."

Michael chuckled. "Something went *bing!* in my heart that night, too. But I had *such* a confused and inaccurate idea of who you were here," he made a sweeping gesture about the spacious room, "in this mansion."

"Really? You've never said that. Who did you think I was?"

"It's going to make you laugh."

"We won't laugh, will we?" Sage looked at Alison for corroboration.

"Of course not!" Alison agreed.

"I ... I thought you were the chauffeur."

"Oh no!" Sage cried, while the three of them did, in fact, burst out into laughter. "Why would you think that? I'm clearly incompetent at driving a limo."

"My thought precisely, at the time. And thus, I was certain that it was the better part of wisdom to keep my distance."

This set Sage into a fit of giggles, which was contagious, and it was a good while before they settled down.

In the cozy silence that finally fell about them, a late-summer bumble bee hummed her little tune among the remaining roses, and Alison fell into the moment with peaceful delight.

"Until Anthony's garden party ...." Michael said quietly a minute later. "When you came to Anthony's party, with Tina. And I ... and the sun dimmed in your radiance."

"Oh, Michael," Sage whispered. "Poetry!"

"Ummm," Alison agreed. "Lovely, Michael." But she noticed Anthony's discomfort as he shifted away from them, turning a bit toward the garden.

Alison knew well how to read him, but this ... was it disappointment? Embarrassment? Frustration?... she sensed strong emotion from him, but she could not name it.

As if he felt her stare, Anthony stood. "So ... what about that ride? The horses are calling!" He chuckled wryly.

"Yes, let's ride!" Sage agreed. "Though just a few more minutes with our tea while we digest, I think ...."

"But of course." Anthony sat back down and poured himself more tea. "And you, dear, would you like more tea?" he asked Alison.

"No, thank you, Anthony, I'm fine. Though it's such a lovely tea. What is it, Sage?"

"It's my own blend. It's a nice, strong Black English breakfast tea, blended with my rose petals from this very garden, that I harvested and dried."

"Oh, amazing, Sage! Of course, rose, that's the delicate flavor—quite special."

"Would you like to take some home with you? I have lots."

"I'd love it." It made Alison quietly cheerful to imagine this delightful tea in her mornings.

They soon finished tea and all agreed that they'd meet at the stables in a short while, after everyone had changed into their riding gear.

"Fortunately, I had the thought that we might ride," Alison said as they waved to Anthony and Michael at the back door. "I brought some clothes for casual riding. Nothing fancy."

Sage put her arm around Alison. "Casual is perfect. Me too, I don't want to get into full gear. But I'm glad you brought something, as nothing I have would fit you!"

"True," Alison giggled. "I'm a tiny little thing."

"And I'm ... *not!*"

"No, dear Sage, you're a goddess."

"*Hardly!*" Sage laughed.

They climbed the stairs to their rooms where they changed into jeans, western style shirts and boots. Then Sage drove to Anthony's neighboring mansion and parked in front of the garage. Seeing activity at the horse barn, they didn't even bother to knock at the front door, but ambled out to the horses being saddled up. Stan, the part-time all around help, cinched the saddle on Twinkle Toes as they approached.

"There's our cowgirls," Anthony called.

Michael turned with a radiant smile, while Stan let out a whistle.

"You girls is *hot,*" he said irreverently. "Cowgirls, *umm-ummm!*"

"That's enough from you," Anthony warned, teasing.

"Yes, suh, Mr.-Boss-Man. Suh," Stan continued with his impertinence. "Apologize for uncivil and discourteous manner, suh."

"Don't know what to do with you," Anthony muttered.

"You could always fire me."

"No. That's the pain of it all. You're irreplaceable. Warts and all."

Stan nodded, patting Twinkle affectionately. "Especially the warts." He gave Alison a studied look and winked. "It's good to see you, ma'am. More beautiful than ever. Does my eyes good, for sure." He extended his hand.

Alison brushed his hand aside and gave him a warm hug. "Who're you calling 'ma'am'? It's wonderful to see you, too, my friend."

"I took special care in saddling Miss Twinkle for you, when Anthony said you were riding her. She's ..."

"She's the perfect image of her mother!"

"She is that, she is. Right down to the markings on her feet, and even her temperament. She's practically a clone."

Alison moved to the horse's head and reached out to stroke the blaze on her forehead, looking deep into her eyes. "Oh, yes, she is. Exactly like her mother. She has the same eyes. Ah, *my heart*. So lovely to see you, in your daughter, my friend."

The horse leaned her head into Alison's shoulder, and Alison hugged her.

"Ah!" everyone sighed at the sweet—and unusual—sight of the horse showing affection with someone she'd just met.

"We'll have a lovely ride," Alison said softly, then turned to the group. "Four horses? Are you not joining us, Stan?"

"No. My boss-man has too much work for me."

"Nonsense," Anthony protested. "I invited you, you said no."

"Well … that's true too," Stan grinned mischievously. "Hand up," he said, helping Alison into the saddle. "Are you good?"

"I am. It's been a while since I've ridden, but it feels wonderful."

The other three had mounted, and the four of them ambled off toward the open land behind the horse barn.

"Oh, I almost forgot," Anthony said. "Will you be staying for dinner? Clara is so looking forward to seeing you, and said, and I quote, she 'dearly hoped you would be staying to dinner.'"

Alison exchanged a look with Sage. "We hadn't talked about dinner yet … what do you think?"

"I'd love to have some of Clara's cooking, if that sounds good to you, Alison."

"Of course!" she answered, thinking that she'd have to sit next to Anthony in the intimate space of ... her former home.

Anthony called over his shoulder to Stan, "Tell Clara we'll be staying for dinner."

Stan waved, grinning hugely and headed for the kitchen door.

As they ambled along, Alison, as subtly as possible, fell into the four abreast line, on the outside, next to Michael, thinking, if only I could completely enjoy this. Beautiful day, amazing horse, Sage and Michael, but ....

Sage broke into a slow trot, and Anthony and Michael joined her, but Alison let the three of them pull ahead. She watched their beautiful forms, all accomplished riders.

Frustratingly, she couldn't help but be drawn to Anthony on Thor. A massively huge black horse, and—she'd have to be blind to deny it—a strikingly attractive man, his sun-caught silver hair in dramatic contrast to Thor's black hide.

The sight of him gave her a rush, just as the sight of him had the first time she saw him, all those long years ago. Only one more day of this internal conflict, she thought, and then she'd return to her busy yet peaceful life.

But her vexation *would not* be stilled, and she prodded Twinkle to break into a trot, then a canter, and then she passed up her companions in a full out run. She ran across the acres of grazing grass, and tore up to the ridge of the hillside, then along the ridge.

Oh, what power, what escape from the world! Everything passed in a blur and all but disappeared as she moved fully into the moment, releasing everything but the intensity of herself and horse, not knowing anything but the feeling of the power, the exuberance, of the animal underneath her. She and Twinkle were as one, all else fell away, tiny minutiae.

She crossed the ridge and down the hill, nearing Sage's land—she would have to slow. She didn't want to. Could she not spend the rest of her life flying on the back of this excellent creature?

Ah! If only!

She relaxed, and Twinkle instinctively slowed, gradually returning to a trot, and then a lazy walk. Alison reined her around to return to the others. She saw three horses, evenly spaced, on the ridge, now far away. The three riders, unmoving, watching her.

Yes, this wild ride was out of character for her. Or, so they thought. But none of them knew her as she had become.

They ambled toward her.

"My goodness!" Sage exclaimed, "That was some riding!"

"It was," Anthony agreed, giving her a "what was that?" look.

"I know," Alison reached down and patted Twinkle's neck. She wasn't even breathing heavy. "Twinkle asked me to let her loose. So I did."

*　　*

After their invigorating and convivial ride, they returned to the mansion to change and get ready for dinner.

"Why don't you go on up, and I'll gather our things from the car," Sage suggested.

"Sounds good." Alison climbed the back stairs to the bed chambers on the floor above, feeling odd with the strange familiarity of it all, but still ... it was not her home.

Everyone had their own room—even Stan who lived elsewhere. But he stayed over on enough occasions to have a room to himself. However, which room was hers, now? Oh, it felt odd.

She meandered down the all and entered a room that she had always kept ready for any unexpected guest. Adding to her growing sense of oddness, it was much the same as shed last seen it, years before.

She moved to look out the window down at Sage at her car. As if on cue, Sage looked up and smiled. She got their things out of the trunk and disappeared through the front door. Soon she stood in the room with Alison.

"That was strange," she said, handing Alison her shoulder bag containing her clothes and her purse.

"What's that?"

"I felt you at the window. I'd just had the thought, *hmmmm*, I wonder which room Alison will be in." Sage paused awkwardly. It *was* a touchy topic.

"And there I stood, with the same thought, hoping you'd look up and see where I was!"

"Yes. I looked up and there you were!"

"Great minds ...."Alison said.

"Yes. Great minds ...." Sage laughed. "See you downstairs," Sage moved down the hall to her room.

Soon Alison wandered down the back stairs, wanting a few minutes alone with Clara, wondering if she'd be able to screw up the courage to ask her the burning question she had secreted away. But when she got to the kitchen, Michael was already there.

"*Oh, Alison!*" Clara cried, waving the large wooden spoon she held. "Alison, it's ... I'm ...." She stood, spoon aloft, as if not knowing what say or do.

Alison gave her a big hug. "It's wonderful to see you too, dear Clara."

"Yes, wonderful to see you. Don't let me get your dinner in your hair. Here I am, waving a wooden spoon about."

"Not to worry." Alison looked at the kitchen table, noting it was not set for dinner. "Are we not eating in here?"

"Oh goodness, no. In honor of your presence, I have the dining room set for dinner, right and proper."

Alison would have felt more comfortable dining in the casual kitchen, but kept the thought to herself, as it clearly meant so much to Clara to provide a formal dinner. "But you won't be able to join us!" Alison protested.

"That's all right, it's all right. I'll join you for after dinner drinks in the library, if you don't mind."

"I'll mind if you *don't!*"

"That's settled then." With a wide grin, Clara returned to her dinner preparations, while Alison sat at the kitchen table. "Where's our beloved butler?"

Michael pulled out a chair and sat beside Alison.

"Oh, he's on vacation. Rambling around Europe, of all places."

"What's wrong with Europe?"

"Nothing. Of course, nothing. But ... there's a lot to see right here, at home, isn't there? Why go gallivanting off to foreign places?"

Alison chuckled. "Well, I guess I'd be inclined to argue that this whole little planet is 'home,' and I think it's wonderful that he's 'rambling around.' I hope he's enjoying himself."

"Yes. He seems to be," Clara consented. "He seems to be. I think, too, that he's trying to dig into his past ... maybe ... a bit."

"Really?" Surprised, Alison found her curiosity rising. This man that she'd known for years had a past in Europe? "When did he have a past in Europe? He's been with Anthony for decades."

"Ummm," Clara nodded in agreement, sliding a pan of biscuits into the oven. "But before that—and my knowledge is completely imperfect here—he lived in Europe. And if you ask me to tell you more, I will simply be making stuff up, because I know no more than that."

Alison exchanged a look with Michael, while they shared a quiet grin.

"Maybe we ought to encourage her," Michael suggested. "I can enjoy a false story as well as a true one, if it's well told. And Clara always tells great stories."

Clara turned to him in mock dismay. "Now, don't you go calling me a liar. You'll ruin my reputation!"

"A story teller is never a liar, Clara." Michael paused. "A story teller keeps civilization alive," he added thoughtfully.

Alison, elbows on table, chin in hands, mulled his comment over for a moment. "What a perceptive insight, Michael. I believe I must agree."

Chapter 3
Dinner at Anthony's

A short while later they were seated at the formal dining table, including Stan. Alison was grateful he joined them, but even at that, five people at the huge table, in the huge room, did not make for a cozy ambience.

How strange to have that thought, when in the past only a few people at the table capable of accommodating twenty never bothered her. At that time, she could make everyone feel at home in the elegant but cavernous, high-ceilinged dining room. But now ... now that it was not her home ... she felt strained and a bit edgy.

She hardly knew what was being served, while listening superficially to the conversation flowing between Sage and Stan, chatting about the horses, while Michael and Anthony nodded in agreement, but remained silent.

Alison never tired of hearing about the horses, but this conversation was simply another aspect of her alienation, as she had no knowledge of the resident horses beyond her ride today.

Finally Clara came in to clear away the dinner dishes. "Goodness, you all hardly made a dent in my vittles."

Everyone protested vehemently, insisting that they'd eaten more than their fill.

"It was unreservedly a meal to remember, Clara," Alison said.

"Absolutely!" Sage chimed in. "I don't even know what you did with those Brussels sprouts, but they're *amazing!*"

Clara grinned. "I'm glad you liked them. I marinated them in a secret sauce I've invented. Tried it out on you-all for the first time tonight, in fact."

"I wondered about that," Anthony said. "I don't remember ever having them quite like that before. I must agree with Sage, you've scored a winner."

"That makes me glow," Clara sad, flushing slightly as if to prove her point. "Okay everyone, off to the library with you, and I'll bring in dessert."

"And join us, as promised," Alison added.

"Yes. I'll be pleased to join you."

They moved to the library, settling in the comfy, sleep-inducing, overstuffed velvet chairs and sofas. Michael sat by Sage, happy as a lark, Alison thought, to simply sit touching her.

Clara rolled in a silver cart, bearing a gorgeous baked Alaska.

"*Ohhhh!*" everyone sighed.

"Too pretty to eat," Alison protested.

"But eat it you must," Clara insisted. "Or I will be mightily offended!"

"Please," Anthony chuckled, "do not offend my cook! I'm completely dependent on her as I don't even know how to turn on the oven."

"Well, then, we must do as Clara bids," Sage acquiesced, "to avoid Anthony starving to death."

"I'll be the bartender." Stan, stood, stretched his lanky frame and moved to the bar to provide everyone their preferred after dinner drink.

After Clara and Stan had waited on everyone, they settled into their own comfortable niches.

The delicate pastels of light bathed the room, glowing through the stained-glass shades of the Victorian floor lamps. A comfortable camaraderie settled on the little group. Alison found herself relaxing into the emerald green velvet of the chair. She signed deeply.

Anthony, sitting by her in his own emerald green velvet chair reached out and touched her hand. "Are you all right, my dear?"

Alison tried not to tense, but his touch startled her.

"Oh, sorry!" he apologized, abruptly removing his hand.

"No, no, don't apologize. I was simply ... I'd fallen entirely into the moment. Here in this room full of books, filled with all their silent knowing. I gave in to this too comfortable chair, too perfect dessert, and with the removal of the last barrier, this lovely brandy, it's all ...." Alison paused.

"All? ...." Anthony prompted.

"*Lovely.*"

"I'm glad to hear it," Anthony said softly.

"*Ummm....*"

The grandfather clock's deep voice rang out the half hour. The sound of the chimes moved about the room, with a slight echo, touching everyone as if a call to meditation.

"I think," Sage said, as the last bit of chime faded into the overstuffed furniture, the walls, the books, "the time has come for me to take my guest home and put her to bed. You look tired, dear Alison."

"Yes. I must confess, I am. I know it's early, but I'm exhausted. The travel, the horse back riding ... the, well, simply the profound change in my routine, along with this wonderful, lovely dessert and delicious brandy ...."

"Ah, I understand," Anthony agreed, sounding disappointed. "Although I've been looking forward to hearing a bit about your life."

"Me too," Michael said. "Even though I recently visited you—and learned of your fame as an artist in the Bay Area!"

"Oh!" Alison protested, "Hardly 'fame.'"

"Yes," Michael insisted, *"fame!* You've had a number of shows in noted galleries. You teach art classes at San Francisco City College, and well, *fame.* Plain and simple."

"That's wonderful to hear," Anthony declared, thought sounding the least bit strained.

"Oh dear. Can I change your opinion, Michael?" Alison begged.

He firmly shook his head. "Nope, not going to happen. But I agree with Sage, it's past your bedtime, young lady. And tomorrow is another day."

"Yes," Alison agreed. "What are our plans for tomorrow?"

"I thought we might go to the art museum— on the heels of this conversation, that might be your greatest interest. Then there's the Fullerton Arboretum, there's ...."

"Now, that sounds interesting," Alison interrupted. "I like the idea of the arboretum. Spending the day outdoors in this lovely autumn air, first a ride like we had today, and then wandering among plants—heaven!"

"I like it!" Sage exclaimed, jumping up and gathering her dishes.

"You leave those be!" Clara commanded.

"No way. You stay right there and take a well-earned break. You outdid yourself with this amazing dinner and dessert."

"They're going to spoil me, boss!" Clara said.

"You don't seem too pained about it."

"No. Really, I'm not." Clara took another sip of her brandy.

Alison stood and stretched, then gathered up her dishes and Anthony's. "Thank you, Clara. Every single thing was perfection."

"You're more than welcome, dear."

*   *

"Thank you, Sage," Alison said quietly on the short drive back to Sage's home.

"You're welcome. But, for what?"

"For everything, of course. But especially for just now rescuing me. I really did need to ... leave."

"You frankly look a little peaked, Alison. And it will not do for you to get sick on my invitation."

"I won't get sick, Sage, tomorrow sounds too wonderful to miss." She paused. "But that ride today ...."

"You were a wild woman! My goodness, tearing off across the country like that. It was ... at first it scared me,

Thea Thomas – 27

I thought Twinkle was running away with you. Hard to understand, as she's so docile. But then I saw you were completely in control and in your element ...."

"I was flying, Sage. Everything simply ... went away. Twinkle and I became one. That's all. I was perfectly, contentedly, in the moment. Utterly in the moment."

Sage nodded her understanding. "There's nothing in heaven or on earth like a full-out run on a horse, especially if you've bonded with her."

"Precisely."

Sage pulled into garage. "But, hmmm, we didn't sort out anything about breakfast."

"I'd prefer it if the two of us had something light, and then went over to Anthony's for our ride. I'm not used to eating that as much early in the day as we did today, and it made me a bit sluggish all day."

"Done! Plus, with less time spent at breakfast, we can ride longer. I felt our ride was a bit abbreviated today."

"Oh, I'm glad you said that! I did too!"

They entered the back hall through the interior garage door.

"All right then, Fruit for breakfast, long ride, a light lunch at Anthony's, and then a lazy afternoon at the arboretum. Somewhere nice for dinner."

"Lovely." Alison gave Sage a hug before heading up the stairs to bed. "Good night, angel girl."

"Good night, angel Alison."

Chapter 4
She Always Landed on Her Feet

Did she dream? Oh yes, she dreamed. She dreamed of times she'd hoped never to think about again ... of riding side by side with Anthony, just the two of them, that wild, beautiful russet, orange, yellow, vermillion evening, years and years ago.

That autumn evening when Anthony asked her to marry him.

That evening when she said yes, and life seemed perfect. *Perfect!* Which it was, for years. But when it crumbled, it *crumbled*.

The dream woke Alison, and her mind swept into the time in her life after leaving Anthony.

She'd been so proud of herself, picking up the pieces and discovering who she was, not leaning on, not dependent upon, *any* man. She discovered her intelligence and talent, her ability to make excellent decisions. Her ability to find a new, cozy, little home for herself, alone. Well, herself and Miss Prissy, her newly acquired, darling cat. She'd made a full and meaningful life.

Had it been rough? Indeed, it had bee very rough. Many impossibly difficult days—and nights. But there was that turning-point day ... *the precise day* ... she felt she *could not* go on. She'd been driving around, depressed, miserable, self-criticizing, self-abusing, castigating herself for not being able to "keep her man."

When, At that moment, *a light came on.* Wait a minute, she'd thought. *Anthony* had not been clever enough *to keep her*!

It had been an astounding a-*ha!* Accompanied by the thought, as she'd reminded herself, that she was not in desperate straits, like so many women for whom relationships had come to an end. Anthony made sure she'd always be financially comfortable.

But money wasn't everything. Much more important than money was one's sense of self. One's belief in oneself. *Liking* oneself.

Returning to the present moment, in the dusky night in one of Sage's numerous guest rooms, Alison continued her deep reflections of the past that her dream had stirred up. She turned in the bed to look out the window, studying the fathomless darkness of the night sky, contemplating the far off stars, burning their wondrous light at unimaginable distances, reaching her, in this deliciously cozy bed as but a twinkling, comforting, jumbled-up string of tiny lights.

In this cozy moment, she recalled *that* moment, years ago, that sweet, small moment, like a twinkling dot of light, that had shifted everything in her. On that dark, intolerable day, she'd driven onto a little street without a clue where she had come, and found herself surrounded by charming little shops out of a Dickens novel.

She'd parked and wandered along the sidewalk, looking into windows, everything enchanting, beguiling. She came upon an adorable bookshop, even more out of the pages of a Dickens novel than the rest. It dared her to pass it by. She could not resist its charm. She stepped inside.

The patrons in the crowded, tiny, bookshop sat in mismatched-but-inviting old overstuffed chairs, and they stood in the aisles, oblivious of anyone trying to get by in the narrow, book-jammed aisles. Everyone with their collective noses in collective books.

Alison felt a smile grow on her face and in her heart as she wandered about. The calmness of everyone so entirely *in the moment* bathed her heart with healing. *Life held promise, life was thrilling.*

There was so much to live for!

She had come to a revolving greeting card rack, filled with cards of lovely pastel drawings, accompanied by compelling sayings.

One struck her to her core, buoying her into the metaphorical clouds. It depicted a young woman, in the air, floating to the ground. Alongside the woman it read:

She
    Always
        Landed
            On
                Her
                    Feet

Alison bought the card. It became her private mantra from that moment forward. Whenever she felt compromised, unsure, or even unsafe, she'd bring the beautiful downward floating woman to mind and say to herself:

She

Always

Landed

On

Her

Feet

In *this* moment, that stirred up the pain of *that* moment, with the added pain and mystery of Anthony apparently having intended to ask Sage to marry him— this new-pain moment, she brought to the forefront her precious mantra.

She'd be all right. She'd enjoy tomorrow, she'd not let wounds—old or new—interlope on her perfect peace and pleasure.

"Thank you darling stars and floating, strong, beautiful, woman."

With that expression of genuine gratitude, she fell into a deep slumber.

*   *

Such a deep slumber, that she awoke to Sage rapping rather firmly on her door. Rather more firmly than necessary, Alison thought as she languidly woke up, feeling singularly refreshed, while still a bit in the land of Nod.

Surprised to see the full, bright, sunshine streaming into her room, she glanced at the clock. It dared to tell her it was *ten o'clock!*

"Come in," she said softly as Sage rapped again at the door.

Sage peeked her head in. "You're alive! I was beginning to worry."

"I'm terribly sorry, Sage. I don't think I've slept until ten o'clock since ... well I can't remember since when."

"I'm happy to hear that my modest little room let you sleep so soundly—and I apologize for pounding on the door. But I'd been knocking in a civil fashion for a minute, and then, I don't know, I got worried."

"Oh dear, that is really unlike me. I'm generally a light sleeper."

"I wouldn't have bothered you at all, but 'the boys' are chomping at the bit, and I guess the horses are, too...."

"Alison leaped out of the bed. "*Heavens!* I'm ruining everyone's day!"

Sage chuckled. "No, you're not, it's *your* day! You may do as you please, which includes crawling back into bed, if you so desire."

"I certainly do not desire to crawl back into bed!" She headed into the bathroom and shut the door. "I want to do everything we've planned—go horseback riding, go to the arboretum, and have dinner at a lovely place." The shower blasted on. "I'll be down in fifteen minutes," she called over the rushing water.

"All righty, take your time."

"Take my time," she chided herself. "I'm taking everyone's time! *What a princess.*" But she couldn't help grinning as she thought of the lovely, precious night, the nurturing stars, the reminder that *she* was the woman who floated gently to the ground and that

    She

        Always

            Landed

                On

                    Her

                        Feet

*   *

True to her word, she joined Sage in the kitchen a mere fifteen minutes later, wet hair, a shoulder bag with helter-skelter stuffed clothes peeking out, slung across her shoulder with her purse, buttoning a beautiful, peacock blue shirt.

"I'm here, wet hair, no makeup, in disarray, but *here!*"

"Wow! You look gorgeous—wet hair and no makeup. You're glowing."

"Thank you. I ... I had a quietly noteworthy night."

Sage, setting a bowl on the kitchen counter, stopped in mid-motion, fruit bowl in hand. "Really?"

"Yes. I woke up in the middle of the night with ... a ... not a particularly pleasant dream. But it caused me to do some soul-searching, with peaceful results. Too peaceful, I guess!" Alison ran her fingers through her damp, light brown hair. "It's like that when you're in a different place. I mean," she reached for a banana. "being in that darling guest room, and the pleasant, but *different* energy let me have some different thoughts." She peeled and polished off the banana.

"Yes," Sage said simply. "I know what you're saying. I've had that experience. New surroundings present new views, both physically and in thought. If one is open to it. What else would you like for breakfast?"

"Nothing! I'm good. I'm ready to go whenever you are."

"*Hmmm* ... not to put too fine a point on it, I had breakfast an hour or so ago, 'cause, well, I was hungry!"

"My apologies again," Alison giggled. "Let's go!"

Within minutes they were pulling into Anthony's drive, and the scene before them was much like the previous day, except Stan had saddled up also, and would join them. The three men were mounted, holding the reins of Twinkle Toes and Magenta. Twinkle neighed and pranced about at the sight of Alison.

"Whoa!" Stan called, "She loves you!"

"The feeling is mutual." Alison took Twinkle's rein. Stan started to dismount.

"No, I'm good," and, proving her point, she put her foot in the stirrup and mounted with grace.

Sage, who had paused, also with the intention of assisting Alison, mounted in one smooth motion. "We're off," she cried, coaxing Magenta to gallop around the barn and out to the terrain beyond.

The unhampered release caught them all, and soon they were tearing up the hillside and along the crest of the hills, the horses in friendly competition in the spirit of race.

Thor, of course, would always win. But they were all surprised when Magenta easily took the lead, and out-distanced them in but a few seconds. Everyone in a full tilt run, flew to the copse of white birches below. Sage pulled in Magenta's loose, permissive, reins as they came to the trees, then let her mount find her way to the little stream. The horse drank deeply, snorting her contentment, muzzle in the brisk, clear water.

The others soon joined Sage and Magenta, sharing a perfect, meditative silence among them, while the horses drank deeply.

Alison, absorbed in the moment as deeply as any of the horses while they drank the living water, relaxed, contented and refreshed, mesmerized by the dappled light on the shining white trunks, striped with the shadows of their peers. The autumn sun, leaning into the south, lengthened the morning shadows.

An errant, unattached breeze blew across her face. She glanced over at Sage.

"The fairies are here," Sage whispered.

Alison nodded. Twinkle raised her head and looked around, her gaze fixing on a point among the trees. "They want Twinkle."

"Well ...." Anthony said, somewhat louder. Thor started, then returned to his drinking. "They can't have her."

Alison patted Twinkle's neck. "No. But they can admire her, and even ... communicate with her if they wish. But they can't have her."

The little group remained in the halcyon tableau until Thor had his fill of water and took his rein to walk along the stream. One by one, the other horses followed, everyone letting their reins loose.

They ambled through the woods then continued to dawdle until they came to a wood-slatted fence that marked the property line between Sage's and Anthony's acreage.

"Home," Sage said simply as the horses moseyed along the fence line. Sage held Twinkle's reins, pausing to look up the hill at the mansion she now owned. Alison took in the strange expression on Sage's face, and read her probable thought—that it seemed most peculiar to be the owner of the vast, elegant, many-roomed mansion, since her aunt's death.

"I ... I've never looked at ...." Sage paused, clearly unable to decide how to name her thoughts. "I've never looked at ... home ... from this location before."

"Beautiful, isn't it?" Anthony asked.

"Ahm, well, yes. I was thinking more 'imposing,' or maybe even 'ostentatious.' Anyway, it's a bit much for one person, isn't it?"

No one responded, but Michael edged closer to her and took her hand, resting on the saddle horn. It warmed Alison's heart to see how clearly he understood her confused, bemused, mood.

Magenta stirred restlessly, and they moved on. They dipped down into the ravine through which the stream among the birches poured, unable to see Anthony's slightly more imposing mansion. Then the horses, left to their own devices, angled back up into the meadow, having turned their backs on Sage's home and headed, if allowed, to their own home—their cozy, warm, hay-and-straw-filled horse barn.

The five friends quietly let the horses have their way, and soon they were back at the barn, dismounting.

Alison started to un-cinch Twinkle's saddle. Stan came over and stayed her hands. "You don't do this, I do this."

"Nonsense!" Alison laughed. "If I can have the pleasure of a ride, I can do the work of unsaddling. Besides, I really want to curry Twinkle ... just because ... *I want to!*"

Stan nodded. "Of course. Enjoy the moment, dear."

As she brushed Twinkle, and everyone else did the same with their mount, she leaned her face into Twinkle's beautiful mane, silently thanking her for the run, for the quiet pause among the birches, for drawing her attention to the other energies in the woods, and for, simply, sharing her undisguised affection for her.

That was the first thing that happened during her weekend that would make it difficult to leave tomorrow.

Chapter 5
The Arboretum

When they stepped into the kitchen to make their way to various rooms to change before leaving for the arboretum, Clara was fussing over a large, woven wooden picnic basket on the kitchen table, caught in the act of filling it with goodies.

"I knew you'd be too late to have lunch here and still enjoy the arboretum, so I threw some things together. I've almost gotten everything packed away."

"You are an eternal gem," Anthony declared. "Thank you dear Clara. Given that I gave you no clue as to any dining here today, that is most kind."

Sage peeked into the open picnic basket. "Threw together? There's an entire blueberry cheesecake in here. And bundles of sandwiches. A veggie tray, with tons of beautifully cut little veggies ...."

"Well," Clara shrugged, "you know me, I'd rather be busy than bored."

"Are you coming with us?" Alison asked.

"Oh, no dear, I've got too much to do."

Alison dared to glance at Anthony, which she'd been avoiding.

"You must come," Anthony insisted, taking Alison's cue.

"Oh no, boss. You know, it's Sunday, and I have certain things that I attend to ...."

Anthony nodded. "Yes, of course."

"So sorry, Clara," Alison apologized, "we're unthinking. It's your day off, and here you are, making us picnics, and being arm-twisted into going with us when it's your alone time."

With a slightly horrified expression, Clara protested. "No, Alison, no-no-no! It's not that. No, I have plenty of time to myself. But, oh ... never mind me, go enjoy yourselves!" She waved them away.

"Let's do as she says," Sage suggested. "I'll get our things from the car, Alison, why don't you go on up?"

Alison nodded, "All right, thanks Sage." She headed up the stairs alone, as the men had something they needed to attend to. She hadn't quite understood what they were engaged in, as she found her mind caught up with the reverie that had started among the copse of fairy-occupied trees.

She revisited the sense she'd had that Twinkle and the animate energy were communing in an entirely different dimension from the mundane three dimensions that she, and other mere mortals, were generally tied to.

She wandered into the room she'd claimed for herself the day before, musing so intently that she hardly realized she'd entered the room.

"Here you go," Sage chirped.

Startled out of her trance state, Alison, jumped nearly out of her skin.

"Oh, I'm *sorry*, Alison, I didn't mean to startle you!"

"Goodness, Sage, I was really lost in the woods!"

"It's the fairies," they exclaimed together, then, having surprised themselves, they fell into uncontrollable giggles. "Oh, jeez, it's not *that* funny!" Sage gasped.

"Still! The fairies!" Alison answered.

"What's so funny?" Anthony paused in the doorway, Michael looking over his shoulder at their frivolity.

"Nothing, really," Sage answered. "Just, you know, a girl giggle-fest."

"Well, I'll leave you to your giggling." Anthony grinned, shaking his head. Then two men tromped on down the hall to their rooms.

Sage hugged Alison, and took her leave of the room as well. "See you at the car."

"Yes." Alison returned to her fairy-musing as she changed from riding gear to a mid-calf length cinnamon and tawny autumn-hued chiffon dress. Perhaps a bit dressy to wander around in an arboretum, she thought, but as they'd be merely strolling, she decided it would do, and she wouldn't need to change for dinner.

She slipped into the little matching bolero jacket, and went down to the Mercedes. Anthony was already there, but Stan, Sage, and Michael were nowhere in sight.

"Goodness! Where is everyone? I thought I'd be the last to arrive," Alison observed, somewhat disconcerted.

Anthony came around to the passenger door an opened it for her. "Michael went to retrieve our picnic fare, and ..." the front door of the mansion opened, "here's our Sage, now!"

"Sorry to keep you waiting," Sage apologized.

"No, no," I just got here myself." Alison continued to stand by the open car door. "So ... where's Stan?"

"He's not joining us," Anthony said. "Clara recruited him for a curtain taking-down project. I didn't quite follow the details. Anyway, it's only the four of us."

Michael came through the front door laden with the picnic basket, stowing it in the open trunk.

"After you, my dear," Anthony gestured to Alison.

"So *ahm* ... yes, of course ...." She got in. She'd now be *tête-à-tête* with Anthony, in the front seat. What *would* they talk about?

"And we're off!" Anthony declared cheerfully.

*　　*

The ride turned out not to be as uncomfortable as Alison had anticipated. After a few moments of quiet chat between Sage and Michael, Sage raised her voice to include the front seat in her lilting chatter. She offered interesting bits about the local inhabitants, some of whom Alison recalled, and some she'd never heard of. All of whom she was grateful to for providing the interesting and *distracting* chitchat.

Much to her surprise, they soon pulled into the parking lot of the Fullerton Arboretum. Even from the parking lot, it presented a stunning array of beautiful plants and autumn flowers. Not only did it suit her mood, but she hoped she'd discover the missing piece to a painting she was in the midst of, that wanted, needed ... *something*.

She felt certain she'd see that "something" this afternoon. Not waiting for Anthony to make it around the car, though he'd leapt from the driver's seat and made he way her door, Alison stepped out into the golden sunshine.

"What a glorious day!" she exclaimed, closing her eyes and inhaling deeply.

"Oh, my!" Sage breathed, "*look at you!*"

Anthony had stopped in his tracks to do just that.

"What?" Alison asked, somewhat alarmed.

"You ..." Anthony faltered. "That little Victorian house behind you, and you in that rather Victorian dress, and the sunlight. Don't move!" He scrabbled for his phone, then took a picture of her.

"Yes, don't move. Me too!" Sage took several shots of her as well.

"Picture perfect, Aunt Alison," Michael nodded.

Alison tittered and posed dramatically for her personal paparazzi. "I need a parasol or a big floppy hat!"

Sage laughed while Anthony protested. "No, simply perfect, precisely as you are, my dear!"

Alison looked around and saw that they had drawn the attention of a few bystanders. "Oh, goodness! Michael, please come and rescue me from myself."

Michael came up to her, offered her his forearm, and they promenaded to the front gate.

"Embarrassing, much?" she said, *sotto voce* to Michael.

"Not in the least! As usual, you've made everyone around you happy."

"*Hmmm ....*"

"What does that mean?"

"I don't know Michael. Just, I'm not entirely ...."

"Oh. You're not entirely comfortable around Uncle Anthony."

"No. I'm not. Surprised?"

"We-l-l-l-l, no-o-o, but ...."

"But?"

"I guess we all hoped it would not be that way."

"Just because Victoria's gone, Michael, doesn't mean the past didn't happen."

"No. Of course not. Of course not. I'm so sorry if you're unhappy!"

"I'm not unhappy. Despite a certain ... thread of ... awkwardness, I'm quite enjoying myself."

"Awkwardly happy. Could be worse. I Guess."

Alison laughed lightly. "No, it's not even that bad. But ...."

"But, everyone please stop trying to put the two of you together," Michael finished her thought.

"*Is* everyone trying to put us together?"

"Do you really think Clara and Stan absolutely had to do something with valances today?"

"Ah. I see. No, I suppose not. I see."

Anthony and Sage, who had carried on their own chat a few feet behind, caught up to them as they came to the gate. Anthony put a donation in the donation box, and they entered the grounds.

Alison became determined to set aside her feelings of awkwardness and enjoy the beautiful gardens totally, with both her mind and heart. Also, with her attention alert for the flora she needed—the finishing touch to her current, frustrating, not-fully-realized, painting.

Sage breathed deeply. "I love this place! Tina and I came to the Summer Solstice Garden Gala a couple of times. It's a big, fun, lovely dinner in the garden and an auction. Great food, great live music. But more than anything, this environment!"

"It's wonderful," Alison agreed. "I can't believe I've never been here. I *love* plants. And right now I'm on the hunt for a particular ... *something* for a current painting I'm working on. Are we going to be fortunate enough to have you as our guide, Sage?"

"I'd love to," Sage said with a wide grin. "If you don't mind my going on about certain plants and flowers. I think it's in my native heritage to resonate with plants."

"We won't mind it a bit," Alison protested, "will we?"

"Indeed not," Michael concurred.

They began at the Mediterranean gardens, where they were greeted by a row of Tree Mallow, a stunning bush with big maple-tree-like leaves and thousands upon thousands of huge, bright pink flowers, that lined the walk against a background of neatly trimmed Portugal Laurel.

The path gave away to a rock garden covered in a profusion of rock rose that Sage pointed to individually, rattling off their names: crimson-spot rock rose, purple-flowered rock rose, magenta rock rose, and others, in a riot of purple, lavender, pink, white, and yellow cheerful flowers.

Their leisurely walk on the warm autumn day was sweet beyond words, and Alison, happily engaged in being informed of the plants and flowers she knew little or nothing about, kept on the lookout for "her" flower.

From the Mediterranean gardens the winding pathway took them into the southwest gardens where saguaro stood majestic, towering over them, their giant candelabra of spiny branches reaching up above the other plants, unmistakably long-time residents of the garden. They, too, were in blossom, their trumpet-like white and yellow flowers seeming to proclaim spring rather than fall.

Other smaller cactus gathered about the several saguaro, parishioners adoring their favorite pastor, clothed in a surprising array of cheerful flowers like so many Sunday morning hats.

But nothing declared to Alison, "Here is the flower for which you seek!"

As if prompted, Sage asked, "Have you seen your special flower, Alison?"

"Mind reader! I was reveling in all the amazing beauty, and delighting in learning so much. But, no, I've not yet seen the special flower."

"*Ohh!*" Sage said, disappointed. "I'm sorry!"

Alison giggled. "Not to worry, dear. You're an awe-inspiring guide, and you couldn't have suggested a better outing. I'm marveling at your depth of knowledge."

"True, true," Anthony agreed. "I, too, did not realize you were this much of a plant pundit."

"Plant pundit," Michael chuckled. "I do believe that must be your title from this day forward."

"*Absolutely!*" Alison said. "You have officially and unanimously won the title of *Miss Plant Pundit*."

"Oh, now, you're all being silly," Sage said. "Plant pundit, indeed. If you're going to make fun of me, I'll be quit."

"No one's making fun of you, Love," Michael protested, putting his arm around her.

Alison and Anthony echoed agreement. "If you stop being our guide, we may as well go back to the car," Alison protested.

Placated, Sage continued their stroll. "I do so enjoy sharing my plant friends with my human friends!"

They crossed into a habitat completely opposite from the one they left behind. A cool breeze bathed Alison as a woodlands breeze rose up around them on their meandering path.

As much as she'd enjoyed the previous two gardens, in *this* terrain she felt truly at home, marveling at the keepers of the arboretum, who maintained the two disparate environments side by side.

"It's amazing, isn't it?" Sage said, "These two opposite surroundings, side by side."

"You really must stop speaking my thoughts aloud," Alison declared, all but shocked.

"Did I do it again?" Sage asked.

"You did!"

"But I think our communing must be a good thing!"

"I'm sure you're right," Alison acquiesced.

Sage continued, "Every plant in the desert environment, and every plant here in the woodlands, are native to the area outside of the arboretum."

"Remarkable," Anthony whispered.

The woodlands garden was a tumult of flowers and ferns and woodlands trees—hydrangea, blue columbine, many-colored anemone, purple alumroot, shy little wild iris, wild lilies, bluebells, happy-faced viola, foxglove, echinacea—dizzying beauty against a background of rhododendrons, sword fern, maidenhair fern, oak fern, Christmas fern, and yet more ferns and woods bushes. All contentedly sheltered by their overseers, white alders, turning autumn-hued maples, willows, and stately oak and walnut.

Practically breathless from the splendor of fauna Alison turned slowly, drinking it all in.

"*Oh!*" Sage cried, looking off into the near distance, interrupting the flow of her descriptions. "I don't see the ducks!"

Alison followed Sage's gaze to a sweet little pond.

"I love to sit on the grass and watch them paddle around," Sage continued. "But where are they?"

"I'll check on the whereabouts of the waterfowl, Sage," Anthony offered.

"I'll meander with you." Michael joined Anthony.

Alison and Sage wandered on through the riotous autumn flowers, their rich hues vying with one another, each demanding attention, while their heady fragrance rose up around them.

"It's a ... wonderland," Alison whispered.

"It is ... a holy land of flowers."

"A profusion of sensual and spiritual."

Sage hugged Alison. "Yes, spiritual and sensual."

They wandered on a few steps, when Sage exclaimed, "Alison, look ... the flowers appear as if they leapt onto your beautiful dress."

Alison looked at her gently billowing chiffon skirt in the breeze. And then she saw *what she'd been looking for*. Her mission had slipped her mind, but now, sweetly understated in a riot of chrysanthemums and delphinium nestled a bed of freesias, in the same shades of russet and golds as her dress, their fragrant, delicate flowers bending over on graceful stems.

She stooped down to drink in their fragrance, and to take a mental snapshot of their delicate beauty. Sweet freesia—*they were what she'd been looking for.*

"Ah! *My eyes!*" she whispered.

"The freesias!" Sage leaned down, inhaling their perfume. "They're so darling. I've always loved freesias."

"Me too." As Alison mentally recorded the precise arc of the flowers' curving stem, the shade of the several blossoms, she noted that the arc of flowers appeared to perfectly overlay the pond in the distance, making it look like a flower bridge. *Enchanting!*

She began to imagine how she'd make the flower bridge cross the little pond in her painting, when at that precise moment, Anthony arrived at the pond, creating the illusion of standing at the foot of the "flower bridge."

Curiously, he stopped at that exact spot, and looked around. Alison knew he searched for the ducks, but she had the strangest sensation of Anthony at a crossroads, trying to decide if he'd cross the flower bridge or not. Torn. Of two minds.

She couldn't dismiss the strange and powerful sensation.

"Alison?" Sage asked.

"My flowers ... what I've been looking for ...."

"Oh! Alison!" Sage breathed, standing by quietly.

"Just ... taking it in. Taking a mental snapshot." Alison finally stood.

"I'm so happy you found what you've been looking for! I'll take a few photos of your inspiring freesias, so you'll have physical pictures to go with the mental one."

"Thank you, Sage, that would be lovely." Alison looked into the distance and watched as Michael pointed among the shadows under a giant weeping willow, its gossamer, swaying branches tickling the surface of the pond. Anthony patted Michael on the back, grinning and the two of them started back to the women.

"There," Sage said, putting away her phone, "I took some shots and sent them off to you."

"Excellent, Sage, thank you."

Sage looked toward the pond. "Oh look, Anthony and Michael are returning. They must have found the waterfowl."

"I believe you're right. I saw Michael pointing to that beautiful weeping willow."

"My favorite tree in the entire arboretum!" Sage said. "And our next stop."

A rush of delight warmed Alison. The compelling fragrance of the freesia fed her inspiration, and the work of art that had languished and frustrated her, would now receive the blessing of the freesia, and the memory of the lingering aroma would put clarity to her vision.

As Anthony drew near, a warm, broad, smile grew on his face—a smile she knew so well when he felt sure and satisfied with himself. In years long gone, she'd seen that smile when he closed on a particularly testy, but huge, financial deal, or when he'd bought a prize horse for his stables, or when he'd triumphed over she-didn't-know-what.

But she'd never seen this smile merely because he'd found the secluded location of a few waterfowl!

This whole weekend, despite her efforts to keep her distance, she'd seen—again and again!—how much he'd changed.

But ... not enough. If he had ideas about her on the heels of "having ideas" about Sage ... they would fall on the sandy terrain of the desert garden they'd just passed through.

The long-ago was unforgivable, long ago. The not-so-long-ago was unforgivable in the present. That he even *could* think of marrying Sage ... utterly, utterly, disturbing.

"We found them!" Michael crowed. "We found your lovely duckies."

"I'm so happy!" Sage reached Michael and put her arms around him. "And *even better*, Alison found what she's been looking for." She gestured to the beautiful freesias.

"Freesias! Of course," Anthony moved to Alison's side, deeply inhaling the freesia's the fragrance. "You've always loved freesias."

Shocked, Alison was taken aback. "I have. But I don't think I've ever mentioned it to ... anyone."

"You did. You told me," Anthony nearly whispered, then became uneasy, rocking back on his heels. "Oh my, look!" he declared, "the freesias appear to have scurried off your dress."

Sage laughed. "I said something similar, except I said they ran *onto* her dress."

"Whether I'm a thief of freesias, or generous with them, I shall never tell!" Alison laughed. She moved away from Anthony toward the pond. "Let's enjoy our feathered friends." At the pond, she sank down onto the yummy cushion of vegetation. She couldn't remember the last time she'd plopped down on a bed of grass, but how she missed it!

Living in a San Francisco Victorian row house had its charms, but her "outdoors" consisted of a postage stamp-sized back yard, filled with a beautiful brick patio, outdoor fireplace, and a number of potted plants, but not a blade of grass.

She used to say it was important for one's feet to touch earth. But she hadn't done it in too many years.

Sage came along and sat beside her. "I brought a blanket, it's in the trunk. Shall I have Michael get it?"

"Oh, no," Alison protested, unbuckling her russet-toned sandals and setting them beside her. "I'm quite content to sit on the lovely grass. More than content."

Anthony and Michael came and stood before them. "Do you want me to fetch the blanket I saw Sage throw in the trunk?" Anthony asked.

"No ...."

"She's quite content to 'sit on the lovely grass,'" Sage said.

"I haven't thought of it in ages, but I never have occasion to sit on the ground. And I feel one must on occasion."

Sage nodded. "I remember you saying that, Alison. You said, 'one needs to be connected with Gaia, and must, on occasion, walk the earth with bare feet, and sit on the ground.'"

"What a remarkable memory!" Alison exclaimed.

"No, Alison. Remarkable teacher." Sage patted her hand. "I've always made a point of occasionally walking in my garden barefoot and sitting cozily among my roses."

"I'm happy to hear it," Alison sighed, closing her eyes, utterly content.

"Your philosophy hooks up like cogs among the wheels of my Zuni mother's blood."

"Ah, yes—attuned to earth. I only met your beautiful mother briefly a couple of times, but *what* a remarkable woman. Just like you, dear Sage."

"Oh, no! I'm nothing like my mother," Sage protested.

"You're *exactly* like her," Anthony insisted. "In so many ways. Which you've proven more than ever by all you've shared with us today. Your knowledge of all this," he swept his arm, taking in the entire arboretum, "is far more than merely by rote. It comes from a deep understanding, a deep attachment."

"Perfectly stated, Uncle," Michael agreed.

"Ahm," Sage said softly, "thank you, I ... I'm grateful for your words, while humbled and, frankly, a bit uncomfortable. So, kindly let me change the subject. Michael, where are the lovely ducks?"

"Hiding out among the weeping willow branches," Michael gestured to the beautiful tree.

"Well, we won't disturb them."

"Nonsense! We shall have ducks!" Anthony began to stride around the pond, but at that moment the ducks came out to the middle of the pond, quacking boisterously, in the jolliest of spirits.

Anthony's three witnesses burst into laughter, as it looked like when Anthony went the opposite way to go around the pond, the ducks came out, having only waited for him to leave.

Michael sat on the grass to cuddle next to Sage, while Anthony returned.

"Your ducks, my dears," he declared, sitting again by Alison.

While the ducks continued their merry-making, quacking and diving, the four witnesses settled into a quiet reverie.

"Look at that little black one, darting around in the pond like he's a power boat!" Michael observed.

"I think they've discovered a swarm of midges," Alison said. "That answers the mystery of why they came out when they did."

Anthony lay back, his hands under his head, looking up at the sky. *Perfectly. Lovely.*

Alison sank into the moment with the gentle autumnal breeze, sharing the moment with the bevy of ducks basking in the Indian summer in their own, paddling, chatting, manner.

The sun sparkled on the tips of the gentle waves created by the ducks, lapping into the sandy shore of the little pond. Alison felt as though she levitated on the unblemished day, cocooned with her thoughts, in quiet reverie.

Anthony seemed to perfectly understand that keeping a particular distance-within-the-illusion-of-closeness was the best way to maintain a congenial harmony, which she truly appreciated.

And the flawless, mesmerizing moment was the second time during the weekend she felt she would miss being here.

Suddenly, one of the ducks made a loud, trumpet-like call, and all the ducks, large and small, rose as one, up out of the pond, wet wings glinting in the sunlight, droplets of sparkling water falling like a cloudless rain. They flew off into the west-leaning sun, and soon disappeared. The little pond rippled in animation for a few moments, but the waves quickly calmed to a glass-like surface, as if the ducks had never been there.

"*Ohhh...*" Sage said sadly. "They left!"

"They certainly did," Anthony agreed.

"That was amazing," Michael whispered. "All of one mind."

"Yes," Alison said. "If only humans could be that single-minded and empathic with one another, wouldn't it be fantastic?"

"It would, indeed," Anthony said. "But I suspect humans do not have the emotional intelligence of ducks."

"So it would seem." Alison slipped her sandals back on and buckled them.

Anthony stood, offering her his hand. She took it and stood, looking down at Sage and Michael, too entirely cozy to be disturbed.

"Are you not hungry?" she asked.

"Starved!" Sage jumped to her feet. She offered Michael her hand and he tried to pull her back down.

"Oh no, you don't. Anyway, big man, you must be hungry."

"Yes. But I'm loathe to disrupt this perfect moment."

"Your beautiful lives promise many perfect moments, dear nephew," Anthony said quietly.

Alison nodded, glancing sideways at Anthony, silently begging him to please stop being so intriguing, kind, wise, and—she hated to admit it, but almost unbearably—attractive.

*　*

After meandering to the car, unpacking the beautiful wooden basket of bounty that Clara had packed for them and spreading it out on a little picnic table, they indulged in a leisurely lunch, maintaining the perfect camaraderie that they'd shared on the grassy hillside.

Alison released the tension she'd felt about Anthony, deciding that the warmth of the four of them together ought not be denied. She left any and all dreary thoughts on the other side of the door stop of her mind.

Be in the moment, she told herself during their casual but delicious picnic. This time the next day she'd be winging her way back home. Back to her "real" life. She had her friends. She had her work. She had art classes to teach. She had the current painting to work on, with the great gift of the freesias, which thrilled her with anticipation. She had a career-making gallery show opening on the weekend.

She had ... well, she had plenty to occupy her life, her time, her mind. *Her heart?* No, no one to truly occupy her heart. But she had a dear friend, a close friend, a friend she could count on. A person who understood her, and who kept her great company. What more could anyone ask for?

"Enough lollygagging," Sage suddenly declared, gathering the remnants of the meal and sorting the trash from the remaining goodies. "Much to do and see!"

She waved toward the Victorian house with its two giant palm tree sentries before it. "*The Heritage House* museum, a Victorian home build in 1894, was brought, every lath and nail, to its present location in 1972 during a midnight, cross-town move, after these acres had been set aside for the arboretum. It's the most darling little museum."

Obedient to their activities director, they helped her pack the picnic up, then Michael stowed the basket back in the trunk. They spent a lazy late afternoon going through the museum, finally returning to the Mercedes with a collective sigh of contentment.

Anthony, hands on the steering wheel, turned to look back at Sage. "Where to, oh great, mighty, and amazing event coordinator?"

"Don't overdo it," Sage protested. "Anyway, it's not what we're doing, it's *who we're doing it with*."

"Absolutely!" Michael said. "But there's no denying that you're a remarkable event planner, dear heart. If not for your ability to orchestrate events, I'd still be stewing around in my soup of loneliness, admiring you from afar."

"Did you admire me from afar?"

"Do I have eyes?"

"Ah, well ...." Sage paused a deep, long, pause. "I suspect we were meant to be together, and neither your stewing in your soup, nor my odd state of oblivion would have gone on for much longer. Though a pity if it had."

"Massive," Michael put his arm around her. "A massive pity."

"So! To answer Anthony's question, we have some time until our dinner reservations—we could take a drive along the ocean, or we could go out to the pier at Newport Beach and wander about, or we could go to the restaurant and hang out in the bar. What's your preference, Alison?"

"Oh, goodness, don't ask only me! What does everyone want to do?"

"We want to do what you want to do," Michael affirmed.

"Precisely!" Anthony started the car.

"Well, I think I might be partial to a drive along the ocean. I'd enjoy taking in the sun setting on the ocean."

"Me too!" Sage declared.

"Me three," Anthony chimed in, as he began to wend his way through the fairly light Sunday evening traffic, and soon came to the ocean. Anthony pulled over so they could watch the sun dive into a calm, grey ocean.

"*Ahhh!*" they all exclaimed, as a radiance of colors shot up through the translucent clouds in unearthly shades of glowing fuchsia, rose, salmon, and coral, sweeping out to a molten butterscotch.

"You could just eat it," Sage said in awe.

"Ummm. *Yum!*" Alison agreed.

Anthony turned to Alison. "Shall I go get it for you?"

"Wouldn't that be lovely! You remind me of an ad some years ago ... a little boy is sitting by his dad on a ridge, they're watching the sun go down. After the sun goes down, in the dusk the little boy turns to his dad and says, 'Do it again, Daddy!'"

"*Awww!* I don't recall ever seeing that ... how sweet!...."

The colors abruptly faded, and the four of them sat in the fast encroaching darkness.

"Well, that was perfect." Anthony sighed. "Where to now, dear Sage?"

"I made reservations at *The Meatless Mountain Goat*. Unless you hate it, I can cancel and we'll go elsewhere."

"I love it!" Alison declared. "I haven't been there in years and years. It was one of my favorite places. How could you possibly have known?"

"I remember."

"You remember?"

"Yes. After I'd come to live with my aunt permanently, you talked about a restaurant that you loved."

"Oh my goodness! How do you remember *that?*"

"Easily enough. I go to it fairly regularly. I made my aunt take me there once, because of what you'd said about it. She hated it. But I loved it. As soon as I could drive, I started going there by myself."

"Really!?!" Alison turned around in the seat to look at Sage, although she couldn't see her in the darkness. "Really! You are *full* of surprises. It would be so lovely— the absolutely perfect end to my weekend, to have dinner at *The Meatless Mountain Goat.*"

Anthony started the car and pulled back onto the road.

"Do you know how to get there?"Sage asked.

"Yes. I must confess, I've been there a time or two myself—and because of the same reviewer."

"Oh, my. I must watch what I say, if I make such strong impressions on others. I can't believe you went there, Anthony. You never ...."

"I know. I never went with you, although you did tell me how much you liked it. But, much like Sage, your talk of it caught my curiosity, and eventually, I went. It fulfills the promise of all of its rave reviews."

"I'm quite pleased with myself." Alison sighed. "And what about you, Michael. You're strangely silent."

"Just listening. Sage has taken me there, and I, too, believe it to be one of the best restaurants in the area. Yesterday I suggested she make a reservation there for tonight. Although I suspect she'd already done so."

"True," Sage answered. "I had. But I loved it when you suggested it."

Alison smiled at the sweet chitchat in the back seat, while wondering if she was about to encounter a dear friend who she'd completely lost touch with, Evin, the brilliant and gorgeous owner of the restaurant. She'd helped him through a very difficult time in his life. And he had done the same for her.

Chapter 6
A Dinner with a View

The car climbed a steep and winding hill. Soon they were in a parking lot overlooking the ocean. A full moon tiptoed into the sky while they bantered about dinner, and its brilliant ivory reflection cast little full moons on the crests of the waves.

After getting out of the car they stood together taking in the view.

"What a day," Alison whispered.

"Not over yet!" Anthony replied as they turned to enter the restaurant.

The warm, cozy interior of the restaurant was fairly busy, but not over-crowded. Sage checked in with her reservation, and as they were being escorted to their table, someone called out, "*Alison!*"

A thin man with large, dark eyes, and an abundant head of black hair strikingly grey at the temples, rushed toward them.

Alison hurried to meet him, and they embraced. "*Evin!* How are you? It's so good to see you! I didn't know we were coming here until a few minutes ago, or I would have called to see if you were around."

"Oh, Alison, I can't believe it. Oh, my eyes! Look at you! You've not changed one tiny bit. *Look at you!* And me, here I am an ancient wreck. Turning grey and ...."

"Goodness, Evin, you're nothing resembling a wreck. And the grey is ... gorgeous!"

"You are too kind. Have you moved back?"

"No. No, I haven't."

"How long are you in town? We must get together and share our histories."

"I'm sorry to say ... *truly* sorry to say, that I leave tomorrow."

"Sad news, sad news indeed. But wait, I see Sage, and Michael, and ... well, Anthony too. I beg your pardon for intruding on your gathering."

"Nonsense, Evin," Alison protested. "On the way here everyone raved about your restaurant. I'm sure they're all delighted to see you."

Evin turned to the waitress, standing by to take them to their table. "Elizabeth, please take my friends to the fireplace room." He turned to Alison, "Would you like that? A bit of fire with a fabulous view of the ocean?"

"Of course I'd like that, but, dear Evin, it's not necessary."

"What about the Patterson party?" Elizabeth asked.

Evin waved his hand. "No problem, we'll take care of them—if they ever come."

"Oh, goodness, no, I wouldn't dream of taking someone else's reservation," Alison protested.

"Not to worry, not to worry, my dear. And, Elizabeth, dinner is on me."

"I won't hear of it," Alison protested further.

He grinned at Alison. "Then pretend you didn't hear it." He gave her another big hug, then turned from the group. "I have a couple things I must attend to, but I'll check in on you in a while."

"Yes. Please." Alison watched him disappear into the kitchen, her heart disconcertingly aflutter.

The four of them followed Elizabeth to a table next to a cozy fire, and, as Evin had promised, a wide open, *astounding* view of the ocean, with its special full-moon-light-show.

Elizabeth handed them menus, while giving Alison a studied, bemused look.

"What does that look mean?" Alison asked.

"Oh. *Sorry*. I'm trying to figure out who you are. You don't look familiar, but Evin doesn't even do what he's just done for movie stars. Merle Streep came in recently, and he treated her like anyone else."

"And I'm sure she appreciated it," Alison suggested.

"She did seem to, yes."

"Well, I'm not a movie star or anything like it. I'm just .... a friend from long ago."

"A friend from long ago ... are you *that* Alison?"

Alison raised her eyebrows in surprise. "I ... I'm not sure. What do you mean?"

Elizabeth fidgeted uncomfortably. "I must go." She caromed off like she'd been shot out of a cannon.

"*Straaaange*," Alison said in a quiet undertone.

Sage nodded, her face in the open menu. "No argument." Holding the menu aside and looking across at Alison she said, "One might think there was more to your history with Evin than .... *one might think!*"

Alison allowed a wry chuckle to escape. "And one might be told not to think so much."

"Yes. It's none of one's business." Sage opened the menu to cover her face again.

"Seriously, there's nothing to think. Years ago, we were ... friends. He was going through a terrible time with his wife, who had cancer. And ... and it was a tough time. We became sort of friends. But I've not kept in touch ...."

"It's as if you're very much in touch," Sage dared to suggest.

"Well, it's that way with some people, isn't it? With some people, your lives take you apart, and when you meet, you quickly learn you no longer have anything in common. And with other people, it's as you say—as if we had lunch together yesterday."

A different waitress came to take their order. Although she gave Alison a studied look, she said nothing other than asking for their orders, and answering their questions.

"Your fame precedes you," Michael teased after she left.

"It's not funny," Alison protested.

"Rather amusing from this side of the table," Michael insisted.

"Show your elders respect, young man," Alison mock-reprimanded.

"Always, dear aunt. Always. Respect, and love."

"That's better," Alison acted somewhat mollified.

Soon their exquisite meals arrived. She, herself, had ordered a mixed vegetable biriani dish, which was as impeccably delicious as it had been when the restaurant first opened, years before.

Evin stepped into the room. "How is everyone's dinner? Please let me know if it's lacking in any way. I strive to always better my skills."

"How do you become better than perfect?" Alison asked.

"Well said," Sage agreed. "The food is perfection, as always."

"Yes," the two men agreed monosyllabically, attention riveted upon eating, not upon talking.

"That's all I wanted to hear ... for the moment. I'll check in again during dessert."

"Can't wait," Alison barely heard Anthony mutter, but she didn't miss the tone.

"Evin has not earned your sarcasm," Alison rebuked.

"And yet, I give it freely."

Michael snorted. "Good one! Although Alison is right. He's a really nice guy, and, I have to say, this is one of the best meals I've had *in my life*."

"No complaints about the food, granted," Anthony nodded.

Alison wanted to ask, "What's your problem?" even though she knew perfectly what his problem was. She wanted to say, "You're out of line."

She wanted to say ... well, she didn't want to say anything, really. Let Anthony think what **ever**. She would soon be home, and this was but a passing moment. One that, if she were to be entirely truthful, she felt more than a little smug about having someone show interest in her, a long standing interest, in fact, harkening back to the time when Anthony broke her heart.

And everyone knew it.

Evin's wife's cancer was breaking his heart, Anthony had broken hers. She wondered how Evin's wife had fared. For the umpteenth time this weekend, Sage read her mind.

"You know, Alison, Evin's wife made a miraculous recovery, all those years ago."

"Oh! Well, that's wonderful."

"But ... about four years ago she suddenly became quite ill and was gone in a matter of days."

"Oh. My goodness. *Goodness!* Poor Evin. So difficult."

"Yes. I believe it was exceptionally hard on him. The restaurant was closed for several weeks, when the employees could have run the place. But he insisted on closing 'until further notice.'"

"Well, I'm not going to say anything about it now, but thank you for catching me up so I don't put my foot in my mouth," Alison said.

"You never put your foot in your mouth," Anthony said. "You **never** do. You're always grace personified. You and Sage both. You'd think the two of you were blood relations, given how much you share beauty and grace."

"Thank you, Anthony," Alison said. "But, goodness, you're being mercurial."

"You think what you see is mercurial. It's nothing to what's going on inside."

Oh. Well. *Hmmm,* I don't know what to say to that."

"Nothing is just fine. Your silence, as well as your words, speak eloquently," Anthony replied.

"All right, then, I believe I shall indulge in some silence, and let you-all come up with the words."

"No words here," Michael said.

"Silence here as well," Sage agreed.

An affable silence prevailed as they ate their dinner. Alison took calm delight in drinking in the view, loving this moment, this strange moment, and the closeness between them. Anthony was, for sure, jealous. And it suited her fine.

The dazzling night, the crackling fire, the warm friendship, the surprise encounter with a dear old friend, all crescendoed to make this the third moment she felt a pang of sadness to be leaving the next day.

Right when they sat back to digest their spectacular repast, Evin came bearing a flaming dessert, followed by Elizabeth with dessert plates and silverware. Ceremoniously, Evin portioned out the delightful concoction into fourths. Elizabeth placed each dessert plate in turn, amidst *"oooohs"* and *"ahhhhs,"* from not only Sage and Alison, but other patrons, as well.

Evin moved to the side of each of them and drizzled a sauce over their dessert, then stepped aside. "I trust you will enjoy my invention. This is a dessert I reserve for the most delightful occasions. Only a few people have ever tasted it." Before waiting to see anyone take a single bite, he left the room.

"You first, Alison," Anthony intoned.

Alison laughed. "Am I the canary in the mine shaft?"

Sage tittered.

"Goodness no," Anthony hastened to correct. "As the guest of honor, not only to us, but to our esteemed—if *annoying*—chef."

Alison couldn't wait. She took a small bite. "Oh, my, that's ... that's ... it defies words. Try it, don't just sit there looking at me. Try it. You must come up with your own description, as words fail me."

They all did as Alison bid, and exclamations escaped from everyone, even Anthony, who, Alison could tell, was loathe to voice his awe.

"What *is* this?" he finally asked.

"Wouldn't we like to know?" Alison said. "But I'm certain we'll not be told. Too bad we can't sneak a little sliver home to Clara. She might be able to decipher it."

"I don't think it would be the same by the time we got it to her," Sage said. "I imagine that whatever this mystical flavor is, it fades after the flame dies. It's already sort of 'flattening,' I think. That's the only way I can describe it."

Alison took another bite. "You're right, Sage. There's something in it that will only last so long. It's not exactly sweet, it's not exactly tangy, it's not exactly firm, nor could I describe it as 'soft.' It sort of melts on the tongue, and yet, it doesn't. It's the most unique taste experience I've ever had."

"I have to agree," Anthony said. "Begrudgingly."

Alison chuckled. "How magnanimous."

Anthony took the last bite of his dessert and settled back in his chair. "Utterly spectacular. An utterly spectacular day, followed by an utterly spectacular meal, in an utterly spectacular venue, with an utterly spectacular view, and most important of all, with the most utterly spectacular, and dearest people."

"Couldn't agree more," Michael said.

"Yes, lovely," Sage nodded.

Elizabeth came to clear their dishes. "Did you enjoy the dessert?"

"'Enjoy' would be inadequate," Alison answered. "'Blown away,' is more accurate. And that's a phrase I never use, but I don't know how else to express it."

Elizabeth smiled. "Yes, that's a common response, quickly followed by 'what's in it?' So before any of you try to wrest from me the secret, I'll tell right up front, I have no idea how he makes it, nor what's in it. He produces it behind closed doors. He has a little kitchen he calls his 'lab,' and he literally closes the door and forbids entrance when he creates this dessert."

"Lucky you to work here," Michael said.

"Not in the least. I've never tasted it. And, quite frankly, few people have. I think there must be an ingredient in it that is *extremely* rare, that he has in only limited supply. That's what I think, but I don't know. Because, given people's reaction, I think he could put himself on the world's map as a chef if he put it on the menu. But almost no one knows of it, and fewer have tasted it."

"Wow, Alison," Sage said. "*You are the queen.*"

"Under the circumstances, I will accept your title," Alison acknowledged. "We ... that's the **royal we** ... are most grateful for this rare gift."

"Very good," Elizabeth nodded. "Would anyone care for an after dinner beverage?"

"I'd love a cup of chai," Alison said.

"Perfect," Sage agreed.

"Yes, yes, chai," Anthony and Michael chorused.

The other waitress soon returned with a tray bearing a large pot of tea and tea service, ritualistically served them each a cup of tea. "Anything else?"

"I wish for nothing," Alison answered, inhaling the aroma of cardamom from the tea wafting over the table.

The waitress nodded and took her leave.

They relaxed with but little conversation, each deep in the pleasure of the moment.

"Goodness," Alison said, "I'm suddenly tremendously sleepy. Poor Anthony, you have to drive us all the way back home."

"I'm up to the task," he said. "Not to worry. But I agree that the meal and the day and the finishing touch of the tea, have conspired to produce a most soporific effect."

They continued to linger, but finally gathered themselves to leave. Alison was a bit disappointed not to see Evin again. But she knew he was busy, and, in any case, it had been *such* a pleasant surprise to see him, as well as enjoy the entire meal and the ethereal dessert.

But as they walked out into the night—after Anthony argued with Elizabeth, insisting on paying the bill, being met with the same degree of insistence of refusal from her, and Alison watching him slip something into Elizabeth's hand, which she knew to be generous beyond the bill, what *ever* it might have been—as they walked out into the moon-gleam night, Evin hurried up to them.

"Sorry to bother, sorry, but do you mind if I have a word with Alison?"

"No, of course not," Sage said, moving toward the car with Michael. Anthony hesitated, but joined them, leaving Alison alone with her friend.

"Evin, thank you! Thank you from the depths of my heart for the unforgettable meal, the incredible ambience and the, well, I don't know how to describe it, the absolutely *mystical* dessert!"

"I'm happy to hear it, Alison. But, more to the point, I ... I ... your friends wait, you leave tomorrow, the clock ticks, time passes." He took her hands in his. "You may know that my dear wife passed...."

"Yes. Sage just mentioned it ... I did not know, Evin. I would have ... you would have heard from me."

"I know, I know. It's all right, Alison. But it was so strange, so difficult. She was here, and then, she was gone. In a matter of days. But, well now, that was four years ago. Feels like yesterday. But Alison, this life, it is for the living, is it not?"

"It is, my friend."

"We can mourn, we can miss, we can be lonely. And we must carry on. We can affirm that this is a strange journey, and make the best of it."

"Wise words," Alison agreed, wondering where his thread was leading.

"I know this is ridiculously forward, and, trust me, it's not my style, but I don't know how else to handle the moment. Might we, you and I, might we find joy in one another's presence?"

"Well, we might. But I live in San Francisco."

"Minor detail. Minor detail. Such issues can be handled, if there's intention."

Alison glanced toward the Mercedes. Sage and Michael had gotten into the car, but Anthony stood by the passenger door, ready to open it for her.

"I ... I don't know what to say, Evin. It warms my heart to see you. And, I did have a moment of disappointment when it looked like we were about to leave without even getting to say good-by. But what you ... seem to be saying, I can't ... I can't respond at this moment."

"Of course not. I understand." He pressed a piece of paper into her hand. "And I anticipated your answer. I've given you my personal phone number and email address. If you're inclined, I would love to be your friend. I mean, I've never *not* been your friend, but I would love to reestablish a connection. Forgive my over ... over enthusiasm. It's in my blood."

Alison giggled. "Don't apologize, dear friend. I enjoy your enthusiasm, and your genius. The thought of reestablishing our friendship is truly sweet and compelling. You'll hear from me soon. I need to get back into the routine of my life. I have a pile of obligations waiting on the other side of my door when I get home tomorrow evening. Let me plow through those, and then, I will get in touch ...."

"Yes, I'll be patient." He lightly kissed her fingertips, and without another word, disappeared indoors.

Alison met Anthony at the car. He opened the door, giving her a studied look, but said nothing.

"*Wow!*" Sage said softly from the back seat. "Simply, *wow!*"

Alison put the slip of paper Evin had given her into her little beaded bag.

"Home?" Anthony asked starting the car.

"Home," Alison affirmed. She felt so dreamy on the ride, even a bit as if she were floating. She wondered if there hadn't been something a bit narcotic in the dessert, or was she simply too, too tired?

No one said anything most of the way home, but Sage finally asked, "Does anyone else feel like they're floating?"

"Yes," everyone murmured.

"Something … *interesting* in our dessert?"

"So it would seem," Anthony agreed.

"That might have something to do with not putting it on the menu," Michael observed.

Alison chuckled. "Clever insight, Michael. No doubt we're extra sensitive, given the extremely full day we've had."

"Full, wonderful, and interesting." Anthony pulled into his driveway. "A night cap?" he asked.

"Thank you, Anthony, but I must go to sleep. And then tomorrow, off I fly, back home."

"May I take you to the airport?" Anthony pressed.

"**Oh!** Anthony, thank you for offering, you are so sweet. But Sage and I …."

Sage stepped in. "Alison and I have a few subjects we have yet to chat about, such a full weekend, we've not had a chance to cover them. We agreed that the trip to the airport would be the perfect time to address them."

"I can't believe I'm saying good-by to you, after such an amazing weekend," Anthony protested, "out here in my driveway!"

"Well," Alison stepped forward and gave him a hug—the first time, other than the dance at his birthday party, she'd voluntarily come in contact with him the entire weekend, "It's not so bad. A sweet and fitting end, under the captivating moonlight, to a perfect day. Good night now, you two." She gave Michael a hug, then climbed into Sage's car.

"Talk to you tomorrow," Sage blew Michael a kiss.

Alison watched as Michael caught it, stuck it in his breast pocket, and patted it affectionately.

Sage drove down the long drive, then home.

"I couldn't be happier, seeing how in love you and Michael are." Alison yawned discretely.

"I couldn't be happier either! But, Alison, I *thought* I was going to be asking you about Anthony. Now there's a little something in the delicious sauce. What about Evin?"

"Oh, goodness, Sage. I have no idea. And, frankly, I'm entirely too, *too* exhausted to think about it."

"I know. No questions tonight. No, I won't hear of it." Sage pulled into the garage. "To bed, with you. Tomorrow is a big day. And I promise, I will not bring up anything you don't bring up first."

"Thank you, my dear." They'd arrived at the bottom of the sweeping stairway. "Are you coming up?"

"No, I think I'll unwind and replay the day a bit with two fingers of sherry. I'll see you in the morning. You're flight is not until afternoon, so please, sleep in as long as you wish. Don't get up on my account."

"I shall do as you bid!" Alison gave Sage a hug and went up the stairs, full of half-asleep and dreamy, curious, feelings.

Chapter 7
Love Poems

Alison awoke in the morning before dawn had even crested. A dream as real as reality had startled her awake, with both Anthony and Evin on bended knee before her, asking her to marry them.

Goodness! Marriage was the last thing on her mind at this juncture in her life. She found thoughts of her work much more engrossing these days.

But she suspected the dream, strange as it seemed, reflected her reality. She then recalled the slip of paper Evin had pressed into her hand, and wondered how she could have forgotten it. But she'd barely slipped into her cozy pajamas before falling into a deep, peaceful sleep.

She reached over to the bedside table, picked up the beaded bag and opened it, pulling out the little slip of paper, expecting to see a phone number and an email address on it. Yes, they were there at the bottom of the small bit of paper. But it was also covered in tiny, impeccably neat handwriting.

Shocked, Alison realized that after producing the unique dessert for them, Evin must have been writing the entire time until they left.

She didn't want to read anything that would make her feel bad, or guilty or obligated, but she began to read, anyway.

Much to her astonishment, it was poetry. He apologized for daring to be so forward, but the poetry had risen spontaneously at the sight of her. He closed by writing, "I hope you'll not be offended by my perhaps embarrassing words. I know I must act the fool in this moment. Because if I don't, I'll much more regret not taking action. *Rather the fool than nothing!*

My humble apologies for my humble words."

Time's Flight
How have you escaped
Time, that curmudgeonly thief?
Ah, my eyes!
Your flowery beauty blew in
And will as nonchalantly breeze away.

Can I capture you with my creations?
No. Nor do I desire to.
But thank you, time, curmudgeonly thief,
For these few moments
With the only other woman who ever touched
The heart of my Heart.

If time had a face
It would desire to change it for yours!

———

And then:

The Lake of Life
Oh! The vagaries of Life
Can push and pull us so
That blindness enters the equation
And Lovers let Love go

Love is why we're here
It's what Life is all about
Regardless of the twists of fate
Love loves you, never, doubt!

The Stream of Life we drift upon
Knows our deepest Heart's Desire
& one day you find your Love near by
Your Heart alight with fire

Love only asks you for your faith
Believe in Love pure and strong
Within Love's amazing Power and Grace
You'll find Love's peaceful song.

———————

And last, but certainly not least:

Still Life with Love
The sun strikes an arrow of light
Into the placid sea
A small blue bench near the water
Anticipates you and me

Thea Thomas – 77

Poised in expectation
The entire scene awaits
For us to give it meaning –
Will we wait upon the fates?

Or will we take action
Moving the very stars above
Seizing Life's greatest meaning
In the Realm of Eternal Love?

Oh wait not, dear Lovers
Even if far flung the world 'round
Rush to the healing waters of Love
Where joy and wonder abound

The little bench is a safe harbor
For all Life may put upon you
In that sacred place with your Love
Faith and Trust remain true

For nothing is more amazing
Than a life with Love complete
A little bench awaits you both
Where, in Love, your future you'll meet.

She read the poems again and yet again, stunned and touched. Evin was a poet in his secret lab with a pen, as well as mysterious ingredients. Her dream of his proposal returned to her, now considerably more real.

She thought back to the time when she'd first met him. *So long ago!* She'd recently discovered the irrefutable relationship between Anthony and Victoria and had been driving around aimlessly, trying to work out how not to believe what could not be denied.

She'd seen the banners and advertisements for this new restaurant which sounded intriguing. Then, curiously, she'd found herself at the foot of the winding road up the hill to his restaurant. So she went. On that first day, she'd asked to speak to the proprietor, because the food was so unusual, so remarkable, she wanted to give him a complement.

But he came stomping out of the kitchen, storming up to her and demanding, "What's wrong with my food?"

Shocked, Alison protested, *"Nothing!* I wanted to give you a compliment. I wanted to tell you it's fantastic. I wanted to say I'll be back. But that's not likely if you're going to storm at me with a knife!"

Evin looked at the knife in his hand, shocked. He placed it on a nearby table, pulled out the chair opposite Alison, and sat.

"I beg you to forgive my insanity! I've been dealing with a lot, and when the waitress said you insisted on talking with me ...."

"You assumed the worst."

"I did. I beg your pardon with a thousand beggings."

Alison laughed. "One begging will suffice."

And from that moment forward, they had become fast friends. He told her every detail of his wife's illness, and she told him the details of Anthony's betrayal. They'd called themselves, "friends through disaster."

Be eventually Alison decided she must leave the area to start a new life, and moved to San Francisco after getting a small art show in a gallery. It seemed like a great place to start over.

And it was. She got over her depression. She had shows in other galleries. She had more work than she could keep up with. There was no time for depression.

But Evin's note stirred up those feeling she'd had for him, so long ago! Not feelings of romance, precisely, though he was certainly, physically, emotionally and intellectually, an eleven on a scale of ten. However, her heart remained shielded. She'd had profound appreciation for Evin, and a true, deep, friendship, with a sense comfort in not being completely alone in the world. Feelings at that time in her life, when she neither trusted nor even *liked* romance, when her devotion to their friendship saw her through the darkest nights.

What did she feel about him, now?

She did not know. He was brilliant, attractive, kind.

He was hundreds of miles away, with a business that demanded his presence.

She simply could not think about it now. She needed to get back to her quiet home and sort through all the unsorted thoughts about Anthony ... and now Evin!

She glanced at the clock. Only six a.m. Well, it seemed like a good time to go back to sleep, and see what, if anything, her dreams had to inform her about Evin on the heels of his sweet poetry.

But first she entered his phone number and email address into her phone, and typed in the poetry as well, all for safe-keeping.

It wasn't every day a brilliant and beautiful man wrote her poetry!

Chapter 8
Rainy Day

Much to her surprise, she did manage to fall back asleep. When she woke up a few hours later, the day had brought in storm clouds, and rain pelted against her window.

She watched it from the cozy bed for a few minutes feeling deliciously lazy, but then began to gather herself for her trip to the airport. She took a shower, got dressed in a pair of jeans and kelly green silky blouse, kept out her light-weight jacket—she hadn't brought any rain gear, not expecting such weather in Southern California, then made her way downstairs and into the kitchen, where she heard Sage humming.

"Good morning, sunshine!" Sage smiled. "Did you sleep well?"

"Wonderfully. I love that little room. Rain or shine, it makes me feel so cozy."

"Well, it's your room, always and ever."

"Thank you, Sage, it means a lot to think of that little room waiting for me if ever I need it."

"Good. Now then, what for breakfast?"

"Oh, I think one of these bananas will do me. I'm not hungry. I'm still full from last night's amazing feast." She sat at the kitchen counter and watched as Sage poured boiling water into a pot of tea.

"Wasn't it just! The *most* amazing feast. Ah!" Sage looked wistfully out toward her garden. "I'd planned on a bit of tea in the rose garden, but that's out."

"However, it's delightful to watch the rain, sitting with you at the kitchen counter, enjoying my tea."

"Yes, it is!" Sage brought two mugs of tea to the counter, then came around and sat by Alison. They watched the rain pelt the last blossoms of the late summer roses.

"Poor little roses," Alison observed.

"Yes. My poor beleaguered roses. But I did manage to gather quite a crop of rose petals that I'm drying."

"More rose petal tea?"

"Yes. And I'm hoping to make incense. I've been studying up on it, and would like to give it a try. It all depends on how I prioritize my ... priorities."

Alison laughed. "Well, yes, almost everything does depend on how one prioritizes one's priorities! Rose incense sounds lovely, especially handmade from your own lovingly grown roses."

"I'll send you some, if I succeed with the project."

"Oh! Could I be so fortunate? That would be wonderful."

"Well now I'd better do it. And!" Sage stood and rummaged around through a cupboard, "I almost forgot your rose petal tea." She filled a tin with the mixture.

"Thank you, Sage. What a delightful treat ... *oh!*" Alison exclaimed suddenly.

"What?"

"I just had an insight. Evin's dessert last night. Part of the 'mystery flavor' is, I think, rose."

Sage wrinkled her brow, reflecting. "Yes. You're definitely right. Rose but *what else?*"

"Maybe … freesia," Alison suggested.

"Wouldn't that be uncanny? That would be uncanny."

"It' *would* be uncanny. And meaningful. I've learned pay close attention to things that seem too intentional to be coincidental."

"Yes? What do you do with these bits of kismet?"

"Watch them carefully, with the affirmation that there *are no accidents.*"

"What about the freesia, Alison?"

"I don't know. But I *do* know freesias demanded a lot of my attention yesterday, and today the scent of roses brings freesias up again. So … I'm attentive. Perhaps it's simply that they will bring resolution to the painting I'm working on. This painting has caused me unusual frustration, simply *refusing* to come together. Or it might mean more. I don't know but I'm attentive."

"*Interesting!*" Sage moved to the door, looking out at her rose garden. "Oh, look, it's stopped raining. Hang in there little roses, I'll harvest you tomorrow, hang on."

"Would you like to do that today? I can call a Lyft to take me to the airport."

"No way! No, I'm refusing to miss a single minute with you. I'm looking forward to our drive. Speaking of which … when would you like to leave?"

"Fairly soon, I think. My plane leaves a little after three, but I'd like to be early."

"Me too."

"I'll be getting home in the dark, which I hadn't thought about. I didn't want to have to hurry at this end."

"That's too bad, coming home in the dark. Who's picking you up at the airport?"

"I'm taking a Lyft or a cab when I get there."

"Oh, no! You make me want to come with you!"

"Well, we could end up doing that, back and forth, ad infinitum, couldn't we?"

Sage giggled. "I guess that's not the best plan."

"I'll be fine. It's just, as I say, I hadn't thought it through. One forgets that the autumn and winter days in San Francisco are shorter than here in Orange County. You wouldn't think it makes any difference, but strangely, it does, at least to me. I still haven't quite adjusted to the few minutes the days are shorter this time of year."

"You tell that driver to take good care of you, or he'll have to answer to me!"

"I'll do that." Alison chuckled, warmed by Sage's affection. "All right, banana consumed, lovely tea consumed. Bag packed, rose tea stowed—I'm ready when you are."

"I'm ready. Let me gather a raincoat and umbrella." She eyed the little jacket Alison had hung on the back of her breakfast bar stool. "I'll bet you didn't bring any rain gear."

"I didn't."

"*Two* umbrellas. I'll be right back." A few moments later she returned, wearing a raincoat and carrying the promised umbrellas. She handed one to Alison, "All right, we're ready for anything!"

They went into the garage, piling everything and themselves into the car. Then, with windshield wipers slapping, Sage wended her way down the drive and was soon on the road.

Alison looked up the hill at Anthony's mansion, hunched under the rain, looking a bit disconsolate and lonely. She tried to shake off the illusion, but it sank right into her.

"Beautiful, isn't it?" Sage asked, glancing at Alison's study of Anthony's home.

"I ... ahm ... it seemed to me, unhappy. Lonely. But, oh dear, I'm anthropomorphizing architecture. That's an odd thing to do."

"Not odd. Not at all odd. I agree with you, the rain, the heavy, dark clouds do seem to make it look sad. " Sage glanced in the rear view mirror. "Hmmm, never saw it like that before, but it's quite ... it really looks that way, Alison."

"I'm sorry, Sage. I've made a negative picture of your immediate surroundings."

Sage chuckled, reaching over and patting Alison's hand. "Only when it rains, and I'm on the road, driving by Anthony's house. I don't think that's likely to affect me much, overall. It does sort of bring up Anthony. But with Evin on the scene, *that* whole conversation has changed."

"Which whole conversation?" Alison asked, knowing perfectly well.

"Well, the first one being where I ask you, 'but *why* don't you fall in love with Anthony again?' Which now becomes, 'so, is it Evin or Anthony?' All of which is not one tiny, little, itty-bitty bit of my business, but I dare to step my feet in it, anyway. 'It' being my mouth, of course."

Alison laughed. But then she fell silent. How to tell Sage what she didn't know herself? "Well," she started quietly, pondering, "I'm not entirely comfortable trying to give you an answer that I don't have for myself ...."

"Oh, Alison, of course not. I don't mean ...."

"No, Sage, it's all right. You've done so much to assure that I got to Anthony's birthday party, you've opened your home, you've been lovely and sweet. And I'm so happy to have the relationship between the two of us reestablished. You deserve to learn a little bit about what's going on in my heart."

"I do not!" Sage protested.

"You do," Alison continued. "But ... I don't know what's going on in my heart. That's the sticking point. My heart is ... confused." She looked out the side window, a blur of rain and trees waving in the wind as the storm raged. "I couldn't be more surprised at the emotions that are raging around in me, like this storm, pelting against the car, blowing the trees about. That's how I feel. It's as if the elements themselves are reacting to my inner turmoil."

Sage kept silent, attention focused on the road. But Alison knew she listened attentively. "What can I say? I'm not in love with either Anthony or Evin. Yes, they are both exceptionally attractive and brilliant men. But ...."

"*Oh!* Silly me," Sage exclaimed. "You *have* someone in your life. What was I thinking? Of course, a beautiful, talented, kind woman such as yourself, is not floating around San Francisco ... un ... untethered."

"Untethered?" Alison pictured her card with the woman floating to the ground, landing on her feet. Sage was surely psychic.

"Well, Sage, I ... I have a friend—Gregory. I'm sure I've mentioned him. But he's ... he's not ... it's not ... we're not romantic." Gregory's sweet face and gentle, reliable kindness flooded her. She smiled warm and relaxed, thinking of him. Perhaps he'd come over tonight. He'd begged her to let him pick her up at the airport, but she wouldn't let him.

He did so much for her already. Besides, she thought she'd be tired and might want to be alone. But now, she wished his always-happy-to-see-her face would greet her at the airport. She could call him, of course, but at the last minute like this? No. "I'm, to use your metaphor, Sage, completely untethered," she finally said.

"Really? Well, then, about these two men, besotted by you ...."

Alison started giggling. "Oh no, now they're besotted. I'm untethered, and they're besotted. What a picture!! I'm floating above Anthony and Evin, torches in hand, hoping I'll float down to one of them."

"Oh *dear*," Sage caught Alison's giggle, "don't make me laugh, I have to concentrate on driving."

"Please," Alison begged, "concentrate on your driving."

They remained silent for a few moments while Sage concentrated on the rain-swept road. "But," she finally continued, "putting weird pictures aside, the questions remain."

"Yes. They remain. I came down to Anthony's party because you begged so sweetly. And ... I'd be lying if I said I wasn't a bit curious to just ... see him. But, dear Sage, why I really came was to spend time with you, and to spend time with Michael. I had no idea that I'd see the blossoming of the relationship between you two. What a bonus! My two favorite young people, finding each other! Yes. Perfection.

"But Anthony? No, it is not to be." Alison shook her head a little, trying to underscore her affirmation to herself.

"I hear hesitation," Sage protested.

"Well, Sage, Anthony and I *did* spend twenty years together. So, yes, even though we've been apart for years, being with him for the past few days, being in what used to be my home, hanging out with Clara and Stan, and, well, everything, yes, it all bears reflection, and causes hesitation. Of course."

"*Alison!*" Sage tore her gaze from the road, to look at her, aghast. "Have I done a terrible thing? Have I, by my childish insistence that you come to Anthony's birthday party, have I caused you pain? Oh, Alison!" Sage sounded like she was about to cry.

"No, dear, it's not that *big*. It's simply ... reflection. I had an amazing and wonderful time. And, furthermore, *I'm* responsible for my feelings. If I'd felt I didn't want to handle it, I wouldn't have come, no matter how much you begged. But I *did* come, and I'm so glad I did." Alison paused.

"It *was* a wonderful weekend," Sage agreed, calmed. "And you discovered the freesias! You'll get to put the finishing touches on your painting. All is not lost."

"Nothing is lost, and much has been found." Alison recalled the strange illusion of Anthony walking up to the edge of the pond, at what appeared to be the foot of the freesia bridge, then seeming to hesitate ... vacillating over whether to cross the flower bridge or not.

What bridge was Anthony hesitating to cross? There was that energy about him the entire weekend. Something in him poised to plunge ahead, while something kept him paused at the foot of the bridge.

"What thoughts?" Sage asked.

"I'm contemplating how the freesia will tie the two disparate aspects of my painting together."

"I can't wait to see it!"

They entered the heavy flow of traffic near the airport, rain pelting, wind blowing. Sage riveted her attention to the road with a few under-her-voice gentle expletives at other drivers. *"Yikes!"* she suddenly shouted as a car zoomed through a red light. *"WHAT* is the matter with people?"

"You mean, besides their general, overall madness?"

"In *particular*, their general, overall, madness. Goodness, please dear, mad people, let me get my passenger safely seat-belted on the plane and winging her way home!"

They arrived at the airport and Sage scored a parking space right in front. Opening umbrellas and gathering Alison's things, they dashed from the car through the airport entrance. Shaking their umbrellas, they folded them up, Alison printed out her boarding pass, and they made their way to a little coffee shop, where they were fortunate to get a small, quiet table.

"This is sweet," Sage observed once they'd settled in.

"Yes, it is. We're lucky to find this little space in the midst of all this bustle." She handed Sage her umbrella.

"You'd better keep it. You may well need it when you get home."

"Oh! Yes, that's quite likely, if the weather is like this here. Thanks, Sage."

The waitress came, and they both ordered the soup and bread special. When she left, Alison reached across the table and took Sage's hand. "Thank you so much for this wonderful, wonderful weekend. You're a pure delight to be around. Please, come up and visit me, any time. Any time! I'm serious. I have a darling spare room on the second floor, with a private bath where no one ever stays, and it would give me the greatest pleasure if you came for a while. I'll try to be as entertaining as you've been, but I doubt that I can."

"Oh Alison, you're going to make me cry. Don't you know that ... whatever social grace or ability to entertain I have comes from *YOU?* Don't you know that, as a young girl I looked *to you* to know how to behave, to be aware and sensitive to a person's comfort?

"As much as we've avoided the subject of my aunt, and as much as I loved her, *still* love her, she was not a good role model. She was ... I hesitate to speak ill of her, but she was cold. And she was selfish. Everything always *had* to be about her.

"When you compliment me, Alison, you compliment yourself."

Somewhat shocked, Alison leaned back in her chair. "Oh! You ... you watched me that closely?"

"Well, as closely as any girl does who adores and, essentially, *worships* someone. As much as any girl who hopes to grow up and be like someone, watches her, and tries to imitate her, yes."

"*Oh ... my!*" Alison exclaimed, words failed her at the thought of having had so much influence over the beautiful, orphaned, girl.

"So if you're pleased by who I am, now would be the moment to give yourself a pat on the back," Sage continued.

Alison sighed, still searching for words. "I had no idea you were so influenced by me. I truly did not. But if I gave you moments of happiness or joy, with all the sadness surrounding you, I'm grateful."

"I was devoted to Aunt Victoria, but she made it clear that I must jump through her hoops, which I seemed never to do to her satisfaction.

"But you! Your eyes always lit up when you saw me. You always said kind things to me. You never, *ever*, even once, were cross or disapproving. Even when, oh, gosh, I hate to bring it up ... but do you remember when I broke that vase?"

"No," Alison shook her head, trying to remember what Sage referred to.

"You don't remember that vase, some kind of a dynasty thing of great value ... you and I had dinner alone, I don't remember why, but we'd moved from the dining room into the library, we were sitting in the big wing-backed chairs. Eaton brought in the tea tray, and he was going to set it down, but there was this vase in the middle of the little table between us. So I picked it up, to be helpful. I had no idea it was so heavy, and it slipped right through my hands. Oh my goodness, I thought my life was over. I was *devastated*."

Now the moment came back to Alison. But she didn't remember the vase. She remembered the beautiful girl crying as if her heart had been absolutely, broken, as if *nothing* could heal it.

"You weren't the least bit angry with me."

"Of course not! I remember the incident now. How could I be angry with you? You were trying to be helpful. The look on your face would have melted a mountain. I don't remember the stupid vase from some dusty old dynasty. But I *absolutely* remember how you appeared to be devastated."

"I was."

"I was only concerned about your trauma."

"But you see, dear Alison, in that moment, while I beat myself up quite severely, I learned so much about grace and, and ... *prioritizing*. You prioritized my feelings above the object. In Aunt Victoria's home, it was the opposite. Of course my parents were, my ... my ... parents were like you. And, living on the reservation ... well, on the reservation, everything was different, in every way. I did *not* come into Aunt Victoria's life with any socialization that she approved of. As you can well imagine."

"Oh, well...." Alison recalled Victoria's rant about Sage, fairly screeching, "that child was raised by wolves!" Even at that time, before the debacle of her stealing Anthony away, Alison had thought that the wolf was in standing right there in her home.

But, as Sage noted, when Victoria made a decree, that's what everyone must appear to agree with. Even if, most of the time, silently, they didn't agree.

Ah! It all returned to the mystery of how Anthony could have *possibly* become involved with her. Even while all of that Alison had been willing to finally forgive.

But that he considered marrying Sage? No. She would not—*could not*—set that aside, though her curiosity burned regarding Sage's part in the matter.

Dare she broach the subject?

At that moment, the waitress brought their lunch, and the moment—the delicate, sensitive, moment—passed.

No, Alison decided, it didn't matter what Sage thought about the idea of marrying Anthony. What mattered was that Anthony could even consider it, and publicly enough that Sage's friends knew about it. It gnawed at the pit in her stomach. And now, even worse, hearing how she'd influenced Sage as a child, part of that influence would, of course, be her interaction with Anthony.

Had Sage always been secretly infatuated with Anthony, because her role model was married to him? Had she always wanted to be married to him?

These thoughts must stop!

"Wow," Sage exclaimed. "Great soup. I wouldn't expect that of an airport restaurant."

Alison hadn't touched her food. She took a sip of the vegetable concoction, surprised at its rich, full, flavor. "Yes, extremely yummy!" She kept the remainder of their precious, short time together in the realm of small chat, sliding behind the slightly ajar door of her mind the heavy, the ponderous, questions.

Now was a beautiful moment. That's all she needed. This quiet, charming, reverie with the only girl who had been anything like a daughter in her life.

Count my blessings, she thought as they finished their light luncheon.

A few minutes later they rose and wandered to the line where Alison would go through security, chatting about getting together soon.

Alison gave Sage a hug. "Listen, if you're at all inspired to come soon, I'll take you to my show. It'll be in the gallery for the month. It opens this weekend, but I'm hoping to have *Freesia Bridge*, which I think is now the unfinished painting's title, done. I want to have it in the show. But that's asking a lot of me. I have *sooo* much to do yet to get the show put together."

"I'd love to see your show, Alison. Let's plan on my coming up within the month." Sage stepped out of the line, ducked under the rope, and blew Alison a kiss.

The next thing Alison knew, she'd walked down the hall to her departure gate, almost without noticing it, and was clicking the seat belt together, leaning back, ready to be home.

Chapter 9
Home Again

It wasn't raining when the plane landed at San Francisco International Airport. The late autumn sun inched its way cautiously into the Pacific, nearly cloud covered and shedding tepid colors. Nothing like the glorious sunset of the night before!

Goodness, was that only yesterday? If felt like ages. *Ages!*

Although she was anxious to be home, and would prefer it not to be pitch black when she got there, as she had a window seat, she let all the harried, hurried people scurry off the plane, then gathered her little bag from the overhead bin, and strolled outside. On the way she paused to call for a Lyft, and scored a ride right outside.

The driver was a cheerful middle-aged woman that Alison liked on sight. She gave the woman her address and settled back, closing her eyes, she bid all thoughts to, kindly, please, cease for the time-being.

But, of course, they wouldn't. *How* could Anthony haunt her so, when she knew it was not to be? She thought of all the times the previous day he'd been solicitous, kind, gentlemanly, witty, engaged, engaging. And, yes, *jealous!* Of Evin.

And she'd kept him at arm's length. How had she done it? She wondered.

All of the images, some that she didn't even realize she'd captured, flowed through her mind, one picture or video snippet after the next. Anthony on Thor, among the birches, erect, elegant posture, perfect image for *Horse and Rider Magazine*. Anthony in the kitchen, complimenting Clara. Anthony at the car door, waiting for her to become comfortable, Anthony at the gate of the arboretum, looking at her in awe as, apparently, the sunlight made her glow, guilelessly taking pictures of her.

Anthony, hesitating at the little pond's edge, with the near freesias creating the illusion of a bridge. Anthony giving her a hand up after the four of them enjoyed the charming ducks, Anthony's beautiful profile, that she allowed herself to steal a glance at, on the drive along the ocean as the sun went down. Anthony beside her in the restaurant, begrudgingly complementing the amazing dessert.

Anthony at the car door, again waiting for her, watching her talking with Evin, then, and she saw it, then he turned away and looked out at the moonlight on the Pacific, refusing to look back at her until she came to the car.

Anthony practically begging her to let him take her to the airport—and her polite, but flat, refusal.

All day she sensed a poised attention from him. She contemplated now what she knew yesterday, but had refused to look at it. Now, she couldn't stop contemplating it. All he'd wanted was a chance to talk with her. A good, private talk. Yes. She knew him well. Yesterday—the whole weekend—must have been so frustrating for him. Never a moment alone with her.

And then she left with, as he noted, that dreary, unsatisfying goodbye in the driveway last night.

She sighed deeply and opened her eyes, surprised to see the driver pulling up to her little Victorian row house. It had started to rain. She'd packed the umbrella away in her roller bag, glad she'd kept it with her rather than stowing it in the trunk. She scrabbled with the zipper in the dark, while the car came to a stop.

"Can I help?" The driver asked.

"Just trying to get my bag open. I have an umbrella inside."

The interior car lights came on.

"Thanks!" She grabbed the umbrella. "Lovely ride, thank you. I don't know how you got here so fast."

"You're awfully kind, I'm sure. There was almost no traffic. Would you like some help?"

"Oh no, I'm fine. Thanks again!"

"I'll stay until you get inside," the driver said.

"Why, thank you, I appreciate it." Alison slipped from the car, opened the umbrella and tugged her luggage after her. She had fifteen steps to scurry up, with the umbrella open and the baggage in tow. Awkward, but manageable.

When she got to the door, she found her keys and reached to put the key in the lock, but the door opened under her hand. A bit disconcerted, she turned to smile and wave down at the driver, while wondering and hoping she'd not left her house unlocked the entire weekend.

She stepped inside as the driver pulled away. Then she practically fainted in shock when the lights in the living room came on.

Karen stood up from the sofa, hair tousled, looking sleepy. "Oh! You're back! Good heavens, I fell asleep. Sorry to startle you. So sorry, Alison."

"Startle? You nearly caused me to faint. And, by the way, you left the front door unlocked."

"Oh, well, I figured I'd feed the cat, water the plants and be gone, but for some reason, I sat down on this comfy sofa and, *wow!* crashed out. Hard work, watering plants," she teased.

"Yes, I know. Well, it's good to see you. Now that my heart has returned to my chest. I love to travel, but the only thing I don't like about it is if I come home after dark to an empty house. I don't mind if it's daylight, but for some reason, after dark, I don't like it. So, it's good you're here. And where's Miss Prissy?"

"She's around here somewhere curled up in a ball no doubt, like I was."

At that moment Miss-Prissy-the-cat raised her head from the opposite end of the sofa.

"Hey, there, Missy!" Karen said. "Right here at my feet the whole time. The two of us like a couple little kittens. Here, let me help you." Karen reached for Alison's bag and hauled it off to her bedroom.

"Thank you, Karen," Allison called after her, plopping down on the sofa beside Miss Prissy. The cat jumped into her lap and curled up, purring.

"Such a comfort." She scratched kitty between her ears and got out her phone, taking a moment to message Sage. "Home, safe and sound, kitty in lap. Thank you, dearest for unforgettable weekend. Hugs, Alison." She put her phone back in her purse and turned her full attention to her cat. "What did you do, while I was gone, Miss Prissy, *hmmm?*"

Miss Prissy responded with a stream of meow-chatter, which sent Karen into gales of laughter as she came back into the room. "That cat! She's quite a talker. She kept me good company, meowing and chattering, clearly complaining that I wasn't you."

Alison giggled. "Miss Prissy, were you rude to our Karen? I won't have it!"

Karen sat across from her in the overstuffed chair by the unlit fireplace. "Tell me about your trip." But then she paused. "Or would you rather I left? You look a little tired."

"No, as I say, I'm glad you're here, despite that heart attack."

With Miss Prissy in her lap, and Karen across from her looking expectantly, she felt quite happy to be home. "It was a fun-filled few days, jam-packed with more activity than you could imagine one person could engage in, in such a short while.

"But to keep you from being overwhelmed, I'll give you a thumbnail sketch of just yesterday. I started out the day with a breakfast of a banana and tea at Sage's, then she and I went over to Anthony's. Then five of us, Anthony, Michael, Sage, Stan, the helping-hand-good-friend-cool-guy, and myself went horseback riding. It was spectacular!

"I rode on Twinkle, the sweetest, most beautiful horse you'd ever care to meet. Anthony rode Thor, who, I believe I've mentioned before, is a gigantic, gorgeous, black stallion.

"We tore around on the land, up hill and down dale. Then we ambled into a little copse of beautiful white birches. It was magical, mystical. Everything was still and yet animate. While the horses drank from the little stream, Sage and I felt the fairies."

"*Felt the fairies!*" Karen whispered in awe.

"Yes. We were certain they were trying to get Twinkle, but we told them they couldn't have her."

"And what would they do with her, anyway?"

"Precisely. Except, I suppose, admire her beauty."

"Of course. Fairies are wise in that way."

Alison smiled at Karen. "I see you've met them."

"Not quite in person, not as much as you did there, but yes, I grew up in the forest. I've had occasion to sense those 'others.'"

"'*Others.*' Lovely." Alison paused, again replaying the moment. The animate stillness. The unseen movement about them. And ... Anthony on Thor, so like a god, she could not deny.

"And then?" Karen prompted.

"And then we rode back to the house ...."

"Anthony's mansion ...." Karen said.

"Yes, to be precise, yes. There, Clara had put together a massive, and, as it turned out, more than we could possibly handle, picnic basket full of goodies. We changed from our riding clothes, and then just the four of us, because Clara had something for Stan to do, went to a sublime arboretum, where, much to my surprise, Sage was extremely knowledgable. She gave us a remarkably good time, naming the plants and telling us a plethora of information.

"The high point for me was when I saw a little something that I think will help bring my current painting together, which has been giving me fits and starts."

"That one," Karen said, pointing to the easel facing the wall in the corner of the room.

"Precisely! My, you *are* observant."

"You're not forgetting how we became acquainted, are you?"

"Of course not! As one of my star pupils—who for reasons I can't comprehend, has stopped painting. I'll never forget my astonishment when I first saw your raw talent."

"*Phooey!*" Karen waved her hand as if to dismiss a subject that she didn't believe in.

"*Not* phooey! What can I do to get you back into your art?"

"I don't know, Alison. I don't have the passion for it that you do. I think about it. But I just ... that's all, I think about it. I'm not driven like you and Gregory are, to actually produce what I'm thinking about. Anyway, I don't have nearly the talent either of you have."

Nonsense, Karen, that's simply not true. You have a genius. Gregory and I have to work at it. Work and work at it. For you, it simply boils up. Maybe that's why you don't do it. It's too easy."

Karen shrugged. "Perhaps. But enough about me. More about your trip!"

"More about my trip ... so then we had our fabulous picnic, then we toured the adorable Victorian *Heritage House Museum* on the grounds of the arboretum. Then Anthony took us for a drive along the ocean, and we saw the most breath-taking and spectacular sunset as anyone has ever seen. We were dumbfounded.

"After we recovered a bit from that, Sage told us she'd made reservations at a restaurant I loved, years ago, that I never imagined she even remembered ...."

"*The Meatless Mountain Goat*!" Karen crowed.

"My goodness, am I really such a blabbermouth?"

"You mentioned it in that interview, remember?"

"Did I?"

"Yep. And the proprietor, your friend, Evin, does he still own the place?"

"He does."

"I'll bet he was glad to see you!"

"He was. We had the most amazing meal. And he, personally, made some wildly exotic dessert that Sage and I are still trying to figure out what was in it. I came up with 'rose petals' and she agreed. But there was something even more mysterious. I think maybe it was something perhaps a bit narcotic."

"Oh, my! Is that legal?"

"Probably not. But it's not on the menu and he rarely prepares it. Anyway, we had that amazing dinner by the fireplace, with a picture window view of the ocean, and a mind-boggling full moon, glinting on the waves. Then Anthony drove us home, everyone in a bit of a torpid stupor. And that's that!"

"Goodness," Karen exclaimed, leaning back in her chair, "gracious, me! Quite the day. But ... what about the *stuff between people?*"

"What do you mean?"

"You've said Sage and Michael, Sage and Michael."

"Oh, yes. Well, they finally discovered that which is as plain as the noses on their faces, and have fallen in love."

"Oh, well, yes, *let's leave that out*, of course! Heavens! And I suppose next you'll be saying 'oh, by the way, Anthony and I fell in love again too. But, ahm, great dessert.'"

Karen's sarcastic hyperbole made Alison practically guffaw. "Nope. Anthony and I did not fall in love again. But he was a perfect gentleman, and contributed to my having a lovely weekend." Alison could not stifle a yawn, suddenly awash with exhaustion.

"There you are, now, drifting off," Karen observed. "And well you should! I'm exhausted just listening to one day of your adventure. Off to bed with you and Miss Prissy." Karen jumped to her feet. "I'll let myself out. And I *will* lock the door. Nighty-night!"

She zipped out the door without further comment, leaving Alison trying to decide if she'd get up and go to her bedroom, or simply sprawl out here with cat and coverlet. She fell asleep before she'd arrived at a decisive conclusion.

Chapter 10
Gregory

She awoke the next morning, surprised to discover that some time in the night, she'd awakened enough to crawl into bed, only slipping off her jeans and sleeping in her silk blouse. She now remembered stumbling into the bedroom, glancing at the clock, which read two a.m.

Now the clock said ten a.m., and she was beginning to wonder if this was her new routine. She'd have to have a serious talk with herself, as she did her best painting in the wee hours, loving to be up as the sun came up. Loving to open the windows, even when cold, to hear whatever birds may be around. They were attracted to her verdant postage-stamp back yard, while their songs, the new sunlight, and the brisk breeze always inspired her work.

So! This business of waking at ten would not work!

She heard the repeat of a persistent noise that she thought was a part of the dream she'd been having about riding on Thor. Yes, Thor. Quite strange. She'd never once ridden Thor, though she loved him dearly, and he was quite affectionate with her, as well.

There! That noise again. Oh! Someone at the door. Exasperating, She wanted to savor the moment. Because when she got up for real, she had to hit the ground running, in order to get her show together and up Thursday night.

She jumped out of bed, mumbling at whoever was at the door, most likely a salesperson. They'd be seeing her dark side, she promised silently. Grateful that all she had to do to be presentable was slip on her jeans, she did so, and ran her fingers through her hair as she scurried to the front door.

There stood Gregory.

"I was about to call 911!"

"I'm alive. It's not easy recovering from several days of too much fun. Come on in."

They wandered into the kitchen and Alison put water in the tea pot to boil.

"Did you forget your appointment?"

"My appointment?"

"With Mr. Styikes, you know, the gallery owner for the show you have opening this weekend."

"My appointment with Mr. Styikes? Today? But ... what if I'd stayed the five days I'd planned to? I can't believe myself, I completely forgot. *Completely!* My phone reminded me of my webinar, but I must not have even made a note of my meeting with Mr. Styikes. Oh, *heavens!*"

"You were going to be gone a *five days?* This week of all weeks? With having to set up your biggest show ever on Thursday?"

"Well, yes, I mean, I don't know. I was in such a rush, getting everything together, I obviously didn't think things through. Didn't I mention I thought I might stay five days?"

"No, you just said you were going to Anthony's birthday party for a 'few days,' and staying with Sage. I assumed you'd be back yesterday, or today at the latest."

"My internal calendar got all crossed up with the last minute disarray of going to Orange County."

"Hmmm, yes. How many fingers am holding up? What month is it? What city are you in?"

"All right, all right, hugely funny. Note my mirth. Ha. Ha. Anyway, now I'm completely muddled."

"Yes. Sorta obvious."

"Okay, am I right? Is the meeting is at one?"

"*Ah!* Alison returns to earth. Yes. At one. And I said I'd come fetch you and take you to brunch, so you would neither have to fix anything to eat, nor drive yourself to the gallery."

"It's all coming back to me," Alison said melodramatically, back of hand to forehead. "Okay, forget this." She turned off the tea kettle. "I'm not presentable, let me pull myself together a bit." She scurried back to her bedroom. "Oh, sorry, go ahead and make yourself some tea," she called.

I'm off my game, Alison thought as she flung through clothes in her closet. What *exactly* were she and Mr. Styikes going to talk about? The show, of course, but the details she couldn't remember. She hoped Gregory had an idea. Gregory and Karen! She had a *lot* to be grateful for in the friend department.

What should she wear?

She felt herself grow nervous, and then decided to let everything go. It wasn't worth it to get stressed. She'd brush her teeth, comb her hair, put on a bit of makeup, and go as she was. Mr. Styikes was used to artists, wasn't he? She could just be casual, and he could just like it. She came back into the living room a few minutes later where Gregory was having a conversation with Miss Prissy.

His eyebrows went up. "I like the thoughtful choice you've made."

"All right, enough from you! I can't fuss right now. I'm still sort of sleepy, and completely discombobulated. Mr. Styikes is used to artistic types. And, although I'm usually all pressed and shiny, this time, he can take me as I am. Let's go, I'm hungry!"

"I must take my leave, Miss Prissy. Your mistress commands, and you know how she can be!" Gregory set the cat aside, petting her affectionately.

Alison grabbed her purse and a jacket and they scurried down to Gregory's car. As he moved traffic, Alison turned to him. "Really, Gregory, thank you so much. *So much!* You've saved me! I was sound asleep when you rang the door bell. What would have happened if you hadn't come?"

"Your world would have come to a crashing end."

"Precisely! No one understands me like you do."

Gregory soon pulled into the parking lot of their favorite plant-based-all-you-can-eat hole-in-the-wall. Inside, they heaped their plates, and settled in at their favorite indoor table, with a view of the beautiful patio, which was their other favorite place when it was warm enough.

Alison gave Gregory a superficial overview of her "Orange County adventure" as he'd christened it, knowing they would probably talk about it and again and again, from one angle and another.

"What about Anthony?" Gregory finally asked bluntly.

"What about Anthony?"

"It's lovely to hear that Sage and Michael are getting together. And it's about time. But you've rather pointedly tiptoed around the subject of Anthony. I'm noticing it."

"Nothing to tell, Gregory," she half-lied. "He was civil gracious, pleasant. A good time was had by all, one might say."

"One might," Gregory replied. "And one might not."

Goodness! There was an energy coming from him not unlike the emotion nearly seething from Anthony, when Evin took her attention.

Oh! Alison thought. *Please don't tell me we're not just bosom buddies, pals, friends?!?* How she wanted to say it aloud, but she couldn't gather the courage.

Was it possible she had three men interested in her in a way she'd steered away from, *for years?* Had there been a little cupid angel in the midst of those fairies among the birches?

She did not like to imagine Gregory thought of her in "that way." She would never, *could* never feel about him in any way other than how she currently did. Which was as her best—strictly platonic!—friend.

Not that he wasn't attractive. He was. The waitress here flirted with him overtly every time they came, as if Alison didn't exist. Which sort of annoyed her, but *meh,* no biggie.

Just for the thought experiment of it, she wondered, *What if I came here with Anthony and the waitress flirted with him like she does Gregory?*

She was shocked to discover that she'd want to scratch her eyes out!

WHAT!?! Where did *that* come from? No, no, no, this would not do! Sleeping until ten a.m. and feeling jealous about Anthony, two things in short order that *would not do!*

Ah! Life could be vexing!

"Where *are* you?" Gregory asked.

"Somewhere over the rainbow," she sang.

"I guess!" He gestured to the buffet. "I'm getting seconds. Join me?"

"Oh, no! I'm bursting."

"Come on. I'm picking up the tab, I want my money's worth."

"You'd lose the ground you made on that score, when you'd have to pay the detailing bill to get out of your car the too-much-brunch you forced on me when it returns."

"Ick, thanks for the picture. I'll be right back."

She nodded and watched him get back in line. Yes. A decidedly attractive man. Thin. Great posture. Brown hair, thinning a little, but it added to his distinguished look. Good sense of style. Deep blue sweater over a button down shirt of a slightly paler blue. He probably dressed just for her. Intense, artistic, grey eyes. Artist's hands, long, thin fingers. Yes, quite obvious why waitresses would hit on him.

And, more important than all of that, he stood out as simply an all around, guilelessly nice guy.

And ... was that not the crux of the issue? She hated the saying, "nice guys finish last." But ... just because she hated it didn't make it untrue.

Her phone chirped. She got it out and opened a message from Sage. "So loved your visit, can't wait to get together soon. I'm sending the freesia pictures again, to make sure you've got them! Hugs, Sage"

Tiny though the picture may be, there were the freesias, with an even tinier Anthony at a distance. There was the bad boy, himself.

No, Alison affirmed, *no!* She would not … no. Anthony was out of the question, no matter what flutterations her heart felt. The whole "Sage thing" could never be gotten around.

"Something interesting?"

Alison looked up at Gregory. "A message from Sage saying how much she wants us to get together again."

"Cool." He dug into his seconds as if he'd had no firsts. "Why don't you invite her to your show?"

"I did. She might come during the month while it's open. That'd be fun."

"It would!" He glanced at his watch. "Ah! Time for dessert. Come along."

"Again, no. Have some for me."

"Don't mind if I do."

He soon returned with a plate piled high with a ridiculous amount of sweets.

Alison shook her head. "One, where do you put it? Two, how do you stay so trim, and here's the big concern, three, why aren't you diabetic?"

"One, in my stomach—go acid juices! Two, generics, and three, genetics. At least, I hope so."

"Me too!" She watched in fascination as the plate of lemon squares, chocolate chip cookies, a brownie, a bowl of tapioca, and some m&ms disappeared.

"Wow!" She whispered softly. "Never ceases to amaze me."

"Me neither. Every single thing was absolutely dynamite! No complaints. Let's hit the road."

"I'm with you."

"Bye," Gregory waved at the waitress as they left.

"Bye gorgeous." She waved. "See you next time. If not before!"

"Right," he answered. They stepped outside. "What the heck does that mean? 'See you next time if not before.' It doesn't make sense."

"You don't understand flirtation, do you?"

"I don't know. Is that flirting?"

"Broadly."

"Oh. Huh."

They got in the car. "Well, it's strange," Gregory said. "Doesn't make sense."

"Flirting is its own cause and needs no explanation."

"If you say so. All righty, Styikes Gallery, here we come."

"Oh, shoot!"

"What?"

"I forgot to ask you, do you know if I was going to discuss anything in particular with Mr. Styikes? If so, it has gone right out of my mind."

"It's something to do with a last minute walk-through of hanging your work, and the lowdown on the opening."

"That sounds good. Everything is already there except this one piece I *soooo* want to get done. It may be a bit wet if I end up working on it until the last minute, which is a recipe for disaster. Be that as it may, I want it there. And I still have to take a bunch of prints. I hope he didn't expect them today. I could bring them later, make some excuse about our having to be elsewhere, and meaning to bring them later today."

"And here we are. Wow!" Gregory exclaimed, "Lookie, a parking space right in front. Unheard of."

"Yeah. I hope that doesn't mean I won't be able to find a place Friday."

"I'll drop you off."

"Are you taking me?"

"Aren't I?"

"We hadn't discussed it. I'm sure it would be a great favor to me."

"Settled, then. It would be my pleasure."

I'm really not myself, Alison thought as they entered the gallery. But I'd better start at least pretending to be.

They found Mr. Styikes in the back room, muttering and gesturing.

"Hi," Alison said cautiously, eyebrows raised, looking over at Gregory.

"Ah, Alison, great to see you." He moved as if to shake her hand, and she extended her hand, but he withdrew his and put it back on the pile of prints he was shuffling. Not from rudeness, she understood, but from sheer distraction.

"I'm putting up your show in my mind's eye. It's a thing I have to do. Do you mind waiting five more minutes while I tie up my thoughts?"

"No. Of course not. I'll be out in the gallery."

"Yes, yes. Fine."

She stepped out with Gregory. "And I was concerned that *I'd* seem strange."

"But ... you've met him before."

"I've never met this ... iteration of him."

Gregory chuckled. "Iteration. Funny, Alison."

"I'm a bit thrown."

"Nah, don't be. I'm here. I'll buffer between the two of you if it's too weird."

"Thanks." Alison pretended to look at the art, but if she'd been given a quiz about what was there, she'd fail it completely.

She'd had gallery shows before, but this was the most prestigious, and she didn't want anything to mar it. It was bad enough to have to wonder if a critic would decide to take a bite out of her. So far they'd been kind, but one never knew when the winds would change, and the critics too.

"Relax, Alison. Everything is fine. Yo don't want to be this nervous now, and again on Friday," Gregory said, standing close.

"No, I don't. I'm trying to use the nervous tension all up now."

"Oh, well, in that case, carry on."

Mr. Styikes came out of the back room, extending his hand to Alison, smiling, then taking her hand warmly in both of his. "I'm back! Putting up a show is my version of doing art. I get quite intense. Sorry if I was off-putting."

"Oh no, not in the least," Alison socially-lied. "I'm glad you're putting that kind of energy into my work."

"Wouldn't have it any other way! So, let's walk around and I'll tell you my plan. I'm so glad you and your assistant are willing to help put up the show. Since Dane quit on me, I'm a bit short-handed. The girls are great, but there are times when a tall person with male muscle mass is really needed.

"Oh! He's not my assistant." Alison turned to Gregory, who'd been trailing along behind. This is my friend, Gregory. I believe you've met him before."

"Oh yes, of course. Your friend. I'm awful with names, which is not the best thing for a person in my line of work."

No, it isn't, Alison thought. "No problem. You meet new people every day. But he is coming on Thursday evening to be of help."

"That's good. Excellent. All right now, her's my vision."

Alison walked around the gallery with Mr. Styikes, and he told her where each of her pieces would go, which she found amazing. She couldn't even remember her entire catalog for this show, and he had it perfectly memorized.

It took over an hour, as Mr. Styikes went into minute detail regarding the hanging of each painting, which seemed to Alison to be considerably overstating it. But she went with the flow, despite how much she longed to get to work on *Freesia Bridge*. Would the freesia bridge make the painting come together? What if it didn't? Well, she simply wouldn't know until she was alone with it.

Finally Mr. Styikes declared everything ready. She shook his hand and waving and smiling, she scurried to Gregory's car, with him close behind.

"Goodness!" she declared as they pulled away from the curb. "Just ... goodness, goodness, *goodness!*"

"I have to agree." Gregory nodded his affirmation. "Quite OCD, but good in his line of work. That's why he's a success. And, more to the point, he makes successes out of artists.

"Don't worry. All will go smoothly. This guy knows what he's doing. Keep in mind, Alison, he's advancing your career. Considerably."

"I know. But is that something I want?"

Gregory took his eyes off the road for a dangerously long moment to give her a studied look. "Don't you?"

"I don't know. I don't need anything. I like to paint. I like people to get my vision, I like to give them pleasure. But I don't need to be … having a lot of days like today. I … I want to be painting."

"Oh!" Gregory said, hurt.

"No, no, not you, dear. Of course, you saved the day in every regard. You woke me up, you fed me, and you got me through this weird experience. But, if I had my preference, I would a thousand times rather have spent the time with you in a studio, both of us working on our inspirations, sharing the occasional thought. Painting until exhausted, then going out for a casual but nice dinner, smelling of paint thinner, with spots of color on our fingers."

"Oh, well, when you put it that way, yes, that's a picture that I quite like. I'm completely mollified."

"Good. Because, not to wound you again, I need you to drop me off so I can get at that painting sitting morosely in the corner. I have a webinar to give tomorrow afternoon, a class to teach tomorrow evening, and then, it's Thursday, and the gallery hanging. If I can possibly pull that painting together with what's left of today and tomorrow, I'd be so delighted."

"Of course, Alison! I understand perfectly." He pulled up to her house. "I'll see you tomorrow night in class."

"Thank you, Gregory. You're the most-special friend." She hopped out of the car, ran up the stairs, and turned to wave to him.

He waved back, smiling, and she was able to release any guilt waiting to leap into the middle of her emotional terrain.

"Finally! Miss Prissy, where are you, I need my muse!"

*　*

Alison was soon in her favorite painting gear—an over-sized man's plaid flannel shirt she bought on a whim, thinking it might be comfortable to paint in, and had worn it well beyond its life span, with holes in its elbows and the sleeve ends frayed, with more spots and spatters of dried acrylics on it than plaid. She knew she ought to break down and get another one, but she had a superstition about this shirt. This was the shirt her muse liked. A pair of equally-past-their prime, and massively multi-colored, be-spattered, previously grey sweatpants completed her ensemble.

She'd printed off a large copy of the freesia stem, pulled the easel out from the corner, unveiled the painting—and sat contemplating it, silently for a long while.

Miss Prissy, tired of watching her do nothing, curled up on the sofa and went to sleep. While Alison contemplated, dusk stole through her home, unbidden.

This is what she always feared—that the image in her mind refused to come through and translate into the two dimensions of a canvas. Why was she stuck? What had she been thinking, what had she been feeling, when she first began this painting?

On the lower left, in the distance, sat a farmstead, with big cottonwood trees around a little farmhouse and a big red barn. A typical farm. In the upper right, in the near distance was a cottonwood branch, with a meadowlark perched among the leaves, head raised, singing her heart out. The two parts of the painting so disparate, she couldn't recall the initial fire that had inspired her first strokes, but there *was* the sense of inspiration.

The only way the process of painting worked for her was when she felt that spark, and she didn't have to think, she simply had to paint. As if inspiration came from outside her head, her brain, her body, except for her hand, which did as it was bid from—wherever the muse resided.

She had to release something. Something was holding onto her muse. What? *And why?*

Then, suddenly, it struck, and she felt it, she understood it. Inspiration sang through her hand, through her fingers. First, the painting needed the pond to be bigger, tying the near cottonwood tree to the far farmstead.

And then came the freesia bridge over the pond. It reached from under the meadowlark's cottonwood branch, arching away to cross the pond, coming down near the front door of the little farmhouse in the distance. The bridge would "bridge" the disparate dimensions, the near meadowlark, the far farm.

It was a perfect uniting, the freesia bridge over the little pond. And what about the tiny man, the figure of Anthony? She put him at the far end of the freesia bridge, looking as if he would step upon it.

Once she started, it quickly poured out of her. She was glad the painting was in acrylics, the perfect medium for this project. By the time she had it nearly done, she, and her palette, were a mass of grey-green of the pond, and russets and golds of the autumn freesias.

Hours later she moved back from her work. *It was beautiful!* And it touched the strings of her heart. Something about it was so evocative, so real, though she'd never been to this place in her life.

When the inspiration had first struck her, months and months before, she'd studied both cottonwood trees and little farmhouses, never having had either in her own personal life.

She glanced at the clock. 11:30 p.m.! She hadn't stirred from the painting since early evening. She made several circuits around the house, her indoor walk, around and around until she'd accomplished a couple thousand steps, not looking at the painting, getting in critiquing mode. Finally she came back to the painting.

Still amazing! It held pathos and comfort, longing and peace—*somehow!*

"Thank you Muse. I don't quite know who you are, or how you can direct my actions, but thank you for letting me create this beautiful place."

It needed some bits of touch-up and finalizing. She would do that tomorrow. For now, she'd sleep the sleep of the just and the humble, filled with gratitude.

"Come along, Miss Prissy," she called to her cat, who had come to sit by her for the last few hours, rapt in the energy flowing from her mistress. "Let's get some sleep."

Chapter 11
The Freesia Bridge

When Alison woke up the next morning, she rolled over and looked at the clock.

Five-thirty—now that was more like the Alison she knew! It was still dark. Miss Prissy's furry little grey body curled up beside her, sleeping soundly. She hated to disturb her, but she needed to stretch fully, luxuriously, trying to recall why she felt particularly delicious.

And then she remembered. The painting! Excited while at the same time filled with apprehension, she went into the living room and turned on all the lights, deliberately not looking at the painting. She had to gather her thoughts, her critical eye.

She had to brace herself, in case the painting was not as it seemed the night before. In the heat of creation, things looked one way. In the cold light of day—or living room lights—sometimes work looked less remarkable. She needed to steel herself against that possibility.

Finally she looked at the painting.

And ... it was still there, that ... something. That wonderful something. The indefinable emotion came right off the painting. The welling up of emotion grew in her and she wondered again where it came from. Quite strange—an acutely strong emotion, but not exactly hers.

She went up to it and studied the details that she'd told herself the night before needed to be attended to, but now it seemed more complete than she'd thought. Just a few brush strokes, and it would be ready for her opening.

Her opening! Given how over-the-top detail-oriented Mr. Styikes had been the day before, would he be receptive to another piece being added after the last minute?

What to do? She now felt an urgency about Freesia Bridge being in the show. It simply *had* to be there.

She took a picture of the painting to send to Mr. Styikes, and wrote:

> *Dear Mr. Styikes,*
>
> *This is the painting I told you about. I was able to finish it last night, and am quite pleased with it. I know you have a lovely and precise plan for my show, but I do hope we'll be able to find a place for this, my most recent work,* **Freesia Bridge***.*
>
> *It measures thirty-six inches wide by twenty-eight inches tall. I'll see you tomorrow with this painting in hand, as well as the remaining prints.*
> *Thank you!*
> *Alison*

She began to make the few small touch-ups to the painting, feeling nervous, knowing it would be hours before she'd hear back from Mr. Styikes, reminding herself that she simply had to be all right with whatever he said. It may be her show, but it was *his* gallery.

Surprisingly, though, her phone chirped but a few minutes later with Mr. Styikes reply:

> *Evocative, dear Alison. If it looks anything like it looks in this small picture, I think* **Freesia Bridge** *might need to be the center of your show. The wall where I'd planned to put your two images,* **"Houses in Rose,"** *and* **"Horse Dreams,"** *I believe, I'll place elsewhere, and put this image on the wall, alone.*
>
> *Everyone, I feel certain, will exclaim, when they see this dynamic image on that large, plain wall.*
> *Good work!*
> *Edwin Styikes*

"Edwin," Alison said aloud. "His first name is Edwin, Miss Prissy. I've raised in his esteem for him to reveal his first name." She stopped working on the painting. It was perfect. The only thing that could happen now was she could fuss with it until she messed it up.

She cleaned her brushes and the area thoroughly, had some fruit for breakfast, then tore around, cleaning up her home and herself, pulled herself together to be the guest artist on the one-hour webinar—her excuse for coming back from Orange County when she did, and *thank goodness!*—after which she got ready for her class at City College. Her sub that she just remembered having requested would be surprised to see her coming through the door!

*   *

When she got to class, she didn't feel like lecturing. She felt like telling everyone to let their muse take over, no judgment, no criticism. And that's exactly what she *did* say. While she wandered around the room, observing what people came up with, no holds barred, she chatted about the desire of their muse to create, and to simply let it come through.

She wished Karen was in the class, she'd produce something amazing. Unhappily, half the class sat staring at the wall, unable to come up with anything without specific direction. With the other half of the class, much of it was uninspiring, while some of it was pretty good. Gregory produced a still life from memory, demonstrating a notable technical proficiency.

"I hope you'll all come to my opening Friday night at the Styikes Gallery. I have these beautiful invitations Mr. Styikes printed up, please take one. You don't need the invitation to come. You're my students, you're invited! But the cards are rather nice. Of all my work, I'm not sure why he chose this image, but it's not for me to wonder. Are any of you planning on coming?"

"Yes, yes," the class chorused. Somewhat surprised, Alison felt suddenly shy.

"Well, I ... I'm flattered," she said quietly, glancing at Gregory, who gave her a big grin, and a thumbs up.

He walked her to her car after class. "All set for tomorrow?" She knew he meant, but was careful enough not to ask directly, "how's the new painting?"

"Yes. All set. The new work came together. I hope you like it."

"I like everything you do, Alison. I just can't afford it."

"I'll give you a signed giclee from this show. Which reminds me, I need to make prints of *Freesia Bridge* in case it sells."

Gregory nodded. "Well, I can't wait to see it." They came to her car. "I know you've got a lot to put together and think about tonight, so off you go. I'll pick you up tomorrow around five-thirty-ish."

"I need to be at the gallery by six, so that sounds perfect. Thanks again, for all your help, Gregory."

"It's what I live for," he said with his usual grin and edge of sarcasm.

She waved and smiled as she drove out of the parking lot, wishing the teasing sarcasm was true, but fearing it a cover-up.

*   *

The next day she puttered around, sorting through her prints having previously decided to be particular about which prints she'd offer at this show. She decided not to have prints available for every painting. She wanted to sell some of the originals, despite how attached she'd become. The objective was, after all, to sell her work. She put everything but "the" painting by the front door, ready to load when Gregory came.

"I've been anticipating this moment all day," Gregory said when he came to the door. "Lead me to *Freesia Bridge*."

Wordlessly, Alison nodded and led him into the living room where the painting stood on its easel, the overhead spotlight on it. She watched Gregory as he took it in, cocking his head.

"So?" she finally said, not able to stand his silence any longer.

"It's stunning, Alison. It's ... it's really ... there's something in it that simply calls to you. I don't know how to explain it, exactly. But it's wonderful."

"Thank you, Gregory. I don't know where the inspiration came from. It looks like a place I must have been, but I've never been to a place like this. My muse took over."

"It's hypnotizing."

"Hmmm, I guess there are worse things than hypnotizing one's friends," Alison laughed, happy that *Freesia Bridge* invoked this response from Gregory.

He pulled his gaze away from the painting. "How fragile is it?"

"Not too, but still I want to take every precaution. I think if I sit in the back holding it, that would be best."

"Agreed. Okay, I'll take down all the stuff by the door. You wait here. When I'm done with that, I'll come and get the painting, so you don't have to go down the steps holding it. It'll be a lot easier for me, I'm taller and my arms are longer."

"Excellent. I had that same thought."

Gregory ran up and down the stairs, and before long Alison was sitting in the back seat, holding her work as Gregory drove to the gallery.

"What do you think Mr. Styikes is going to think of this work, and where do you think he'll hang it, with all how repressed he is," Gregory asked on the way.

"I messaged him yesterday with a little photo of it, ready to wait *hours* before hearing from him. Bracing myself if he said, 'I'm sorry, but there's no space for another work.' But he zinged back to me in minutes, saying he loved the work, and he was going to make it the center piece of the show if it looked in person like it appeared in the tiny photo. I'm sure it's much better live."

"No doubt. Well, that's pretty special, then, isn't it?"

"Yes. And even more special, he signed his message with his entire name."

"Oh wow, you're in now, aren't you? Is it urban legend, or is it true that he doesn't let anyone know his first name without being in his inner circle?"

"I don't know. But I'm keeping my mouth shut, in any event."

"Not even going to tell me?"

"Nope. You'll have to earn it on your own."

"That'll be the day!"

They came to the gallery and, once again, Gregory got a parking spot right in front. "Am I having phenomenal luck?"

"Uncanny luck. It does seen as though energies are in our favor. Or brace yourself for tomorrow."

"Right. Now you stay put, I'll come around and get the painting, you climb out. When we get you and the painting safely inside, I'll come get the prints."

"You're so organized," Alison exclaimed. "You beat my abilities all over the place."

"Oh, I don't know about that," he said shyly. "But—thanks!" He jumped out of the car and ran around to the passenger side, carefully took the painting while Alison got out, then they went into the gallery.

Mr. Styikes had been watching from the front window. "Oh, be careful, ahm ..."

"Gregory," Gregory supplied.

"Yes, of course, Gregory. Sorry. I'm terrible with names. Gave me the willies to watch your beautiful work exposed like that."

"I'm fortunate that Gregory was able to drive me here, and carry the painting. It's pretty awkward for me."

"Of course," Mr. Styikes smiled distractedly. "So lucky to have you, Gregory."

Gregory raised the painting just enough to cover his face, looking at Alison behind it and rolling his eyes. Alison knew he meant, "Mr. Styikes, you don't 'have' me."

"Agreed!" She couldn't resist rubbing it in. "We're immensely lucky to have Gregory, it's true."

"Did I have another appointment this evening?" Gregory asked.

"No, no. Nothing other than helping Mr. Styikes and me put up my show."

"I won't be doing much," Mr. Styikes interjected, "other than supervising. But my helpers will be ... helping!" He chuckled.

"As helpers are inclined to do, if they're any good," Alison noted.

"Precisely!" Mr. Styikes nodded.

"Okie-dokie, enough charming chatter. Is there some place you'd like me to set this down?" Gregory said.

"Sorry, Gregory," Alison took the painting from him. "*Sorry!*" She gave him a truly apologetic look, realizing he may not be enjoying the banter.

"'*Freesia Bridge*' is going here," Mr. Styikes led them around to the backside of the freestanding wall in the middle of the gallery.

"Right on this wall. It will be here all by itself. I think it'll have huge impact when people come around this corner."

"It certainly will!" Gregory exclaimed. "That's perfect."

"And what say you, Miss Alison?"

"I can't wait to see it in place. Should we get busy?"

"Yes. First I must close up shop, and then we'll change out the show."

Mr. Styikes chased everyone out of his gallery, except the two of them and his two employees. Mr. Styikes and Jan and Jen, his employees, soon had the current show down from the walls.

"Did a lot of the previous show sell?" Alison asked, noticing that there were few "Sold" stickers on the title cards.

"Not much," Mr. Styikes shook his head. "Over-priced, and not particularly inspiring. Your show will sell lots. First, you have plenty of prints, which will probably go like hot cakes, and secondly, your work is representational. People like things that look *like things*. Don't get me wrong, I love figurative art, but beautiful work like yours moves exceptionally well, and makes us both money."

"Well, to each his or her own," Alison said. "I can only paint 'real' things. My mind simply does not go to abstract visualization. Next, I'd like to get into encaustic. I love its dreamy impression, and the mysterious illusion of depth. I'm not set up for it, but I have a friend who has an encaustic studio. She's offered to let me use her space."

"Keep me in mind if you build a body of encaustic work, Alison," Mr. Styikes said. "I'm quite fond of it myself, but I'm also fussy—as you know. I suspect you'll turn out gorgeous work."

"I hope so. But first things first, and that's to get this show together for the opening tomorrow. I do hope I won't be standing here alone with the two of you and your employees tomorrow evening."

"It'll be busy. People have picked up the announcement cards left and right. There's hardly any left. It's a pretty clear indicator of an active opening. People like your charm as a person, Alison, plus you have so many students devoted to you and your work, they'll want to be here.

"Unlike those artists who are curmudgeons, busy being 'artists,' you know. Judgmental, unpleasant creatures. People may love their work, but they're not easy to be around."

"Perhaps I ought to try to be more curmudgeonly, so it'll seem like a real artist," Alison suggested.

Mr, Styikes gestured to *Freesia Bridge* sitting on the floor below where it was to be hung. "You're a real artist, darling. Now, let's get the show up!"

"Yes, let's," Alison agreed.

For the next four hours, Mr. Styikes orchestrated Alison, Gregory, and Jen and Jan—that, for the life of her, Alison could not sort out which was who, as they were similar in every regard. She kept calling one by the other's name, which she found most embarrassing, as she prided herself on being good with people's names.

A couple hours later Gregory took her aside for a moment and said, "I know this is getting to you, and I understand why it's a challenge, but here's a clue, 'Jen' is wearing a silver eagle pendant around her neck."

"I did notice it," Alison nodded.

"So, 'E' for eagle, for the 'E' in 'Jen.' By process of elimination, the other girl is 'Jan.'"

Alison gave Gregory a hug. "Thank you. Goodness, the whole confusion was taking too much of my mind."

"I saw that," Gregory said.

Alison returned to the project with renewed vigor. And didn't misname either Jen or Jan one more time.

By ten p.m. the show had been mounted, the spot-lights adjusted, and everything in its place.

"Tidy as a bin of pins!" Mr. Styikes declared, obviously satisfied. "Time for our Walkabout."

"'Walkabout?'" Alison asked.

"Yes. After every mounting, those present are requested to walk through the show. We will stop at each image as each of us silently blesses and secures each image. By 'secure' I mean put an energy around it that protects it, while, at the same time, assuring that its true owner discovers it, and that the work of the artist—*your* work, in this case, Alison—will bless the home where it comes to reside."

"*Oh!*" Alison exclaimed. "How ... words fail me. How exquisite. How ... spiritual."

"I love the Walkabout," Jan said. "It's my favorite part of my whole job, working for Mr. Styikes."

"Thank you, dear," Mr. Styikes said. "Now every-one, kindly follow me."

They followed Mr. Styikes as he stepped outside. Then they came through the front door, and in a little group, gathered before each of Alison's paintings in turn, silently meditating on it for a few moments, then moving to the next one.

Alison became awash with the gathering energy in the group, and in the gallery altogether. She didn't know how she'd keep from bursting into tears as she felt herself expand with *Being In The Moment*.

Finally they came to *Freesia Bridge*. Mr Styikes stood there for a long, long time, as did they all.

Alison had never experienced such an event in her life. She felt their minds as one, while sensing each one's attention and blessing of the painting, and the whole gallery of work.

Then Mr. Styikes led them into his inner sanctum, where Alison had never been, and closed the door. "Beautifully done, everyone!" He unveiled a bottle of exquisite champagne in an ice bucket and popped it open, pouring the bubbly into delicate, long-stemmed champagne flutes, handing the first to Alison.

"To a great show," he declared when everyone had their glass in hand.

"Thank you. I'm so ... I can't speak," Alison said, as tears again threatened to erupt. "'The 'Walkabout' has been one of the most meaningful events of my life. I'm honored to have experienced each of your genuine blessings of my work. Thank you!"

Glasses clinked as everyone declared, *"To Alison's show!"*

And then, finally, she did, indeed, shed a few tears.

Chapter 12
Art Show Opening

As Gregory drove her home, she had little to say, between exhaustion and overwhelm. Imagine! People blessing her work in this collaborative fashion, with such focus, such intention.

"It was ... beautiful," she whispered.

"Yes, Alison, beautiful and moving. I feel as you do. Quiet. Spiritual. What potential humans have when they hook up to ... to life's energies."

"That's right, Gregory. You've said it perfectly."

He pulled up to her home. "Do you want me to walk you up?"

"No. I'm fine. Just need to go to bed and sleep until I'm done sleeping. And then, I'll relax tomorrow until I get ready for the opening."

"I'll be here at six, is that good?"

"Perfect, as always." She got out and climbed the stairs, gave a small wave as she stepped inside and went straight to bed, Miss Prissy curled up at her side.

"Good night kitty. May we both have a dreamless, deep, deep, sleep."

*   *

Alison slept well, but it was not dreamless. She woke in the middle of the night with a disconcertingly real experience of having a conversation with the giant yet sweet stallion, Thor. Head to head. Strange and mystical. Disturbing, but also exciting.

Why was Thor repeatedly coming into her dreams? The dream so awakened her that she sat up and turned on the bedside light. Miss Prissy opened an eye and glanced at her, but went right back to sleep. The clock registered three-thirty.

What had the conversation between Thor and herself been? So intense! But now she couldn't remember a word.

Strange. Strange. *Strange.* Of course, dreams were often strange. But rarely so real as real. And now, she'd had two extremely real dreams about Thor, so real that they startled her awake. She closed her eyes and still could see Thor looking at her. Surely this was a visitation from Thor.

Was it something about the show? Was it something about Anthony? Was it something about Thor? Or Twinkle? Was it good? Was it bad?

But the intention refused to come clear, and she knew she needed more sleep. If she got up now and started fussing about, she'd be up until evening, and she wanted to be fully rested for the opening.

She turned out the bedside light and curled around Miss Prissy, deep in thought and wonderment about what Thor wanted her know. And with those thoughts, she managed to fall back asleep.

134 – One Love

She woke up much later to bight sunlight streaming through her bedroom window. Glancing at the clock she feared what it might say. Please, not ten-thirty, she thought. Eight-thirty-two. That was fine. She intended to spend the day indulging herself in *herself*, fussing with hair and nails.

She'd thought of going to her salon, but finally decided that she did not want to leave home. She wanted to spend the day in her jammies, polishing all twenty nails three or four coats of a muted pink, and otherwise relaxing, thinking calming thoughts, and sending good energy to the evening.

As she lollygagged in bed, she mulled over the "Thor dreams." She decided that they were Anthony's way of wishing her and her show well. As she reflected on this contemplation, her phone in her purse on the chair across the room, chirped. Then she heard it chirp again. Others—besides Anthony and Thor—were sending her well wishes. How sweet, although she felt no urgency about getting up to look at the messages.

Finally she decided she was ready to embrace the day with action rather than stretching. She retrieved her phone and crawled back into bed.

First was a message from Sage. At first happy to see her name, her brow furrowed as she read the message.

> *Dear Alison,*
>
> *Today's the big day! I know your show will be an event to remember! Congratulations and I send you the best of wishes.*
>
> *Also, though, I wanted to tell you about a curious thing ... I've found a small lock box in*

a strange location that I was able to open with a tiny key I found some while ago, and had no idea what it went to. In it I found a teeny-tiny, and I mean about two-and-a-half inches by three inches, diary, also locked. It opened with the same key. In it my aunt has written a bit of autobiography, that knocked me for a loop. You may find it of interest.

I'm not at all comfortable putting that text in writing here. In fact, I think a person needs to see the original to get the sense of its peculiar truthfulness. The unnerving aspect of it is that the most significant entry is the last one, dated the day before her demise.

*I know this is the last thing you need to be thinking about today, of all days. But, on another hand, I cannot **not** share it, and I apologize profusely if this disrupts you in any way. I hope it does not.*

Love,

Sage

Well, it rather *did* disturb her, and she didn't know why, of course, since Sage told her nothing of the contents. She decided to dismiss thinking about it further—as much as she could—until some other day. Not today!

But still, what could it possibly have said that Sage, usually exceptionally sensitive to the feelings of others, would dare to disrupt *this* day?

She moved on to the next message, which was from Evin.

Dear Alison,

My thoughts are with you today. I'd love to see your wonderful work in your opening, but, alas, I must keep it as a mental image only. Perhaps you'll take a few pictures and send them to me. I'd very much enjoy that.

But I also must tell you about the dream I had last night, that was so real. You were talking with a big, black horse, and I had the sense that it was Thor. The two of you were having an extremely serious conversation, and the feeling I had when it woke me was that I must retract the overture I made to you. I do not regret giving you my humble poetry. Not in the least. More to the point, I thank you for inspiring it.

I know we will always and always be "heart-friends." I send you a love that transcends the paltry expression of the emotion that one generally finds on earth.

May you be calm and joyful in the celebration of today.
Your Forever Friend,
Evin

Alison read and re-read Evin's message. He had shared her dream, except from the perspective of watcher, not participant. Watcher. She put her phone down and gathered her manicure paraphernalia, deep in thought. She could call Sage. She could call Evin. She could chat with them. She could disrupt her day. Or she could stay focused on the original intention of the day.

She decided for the latter. She knew the two people involved would have her make this decision.

Once her toes had a coat of the lovely pink, she scrolled through her email. Lots of happy notes from her students, and not only the current ones, but also students from years gone by. Some of them to say they wish they could make it, but were otherwise engaged, or had moved far away. But many of them noted that they were looking forward to her show and would be there that evening.

He heart overflowed with happiness. She continued with the various rituals of the day, and in what seemed a remarkably short while, it was time for her to get dressed, ready for Gregory when he knocked at her front door.

She slipped on a floor length pale sea-foam green sheath. High collar, long sleeves, with muted gold buttons along the left shoulder from collar to sleeve. Quiet and sophisticated. She set the shoe box with the muted gold shoes with three-inch heels by the door, along with her Nikes. No, she would not negotiate her stairway in high heels! Nikes for stairs, heels for the show.

She put on the muted gold necklace with a single emerald, and a matching bracelet, encircled by small emeralds, and a pair of single stone emerald earrings, the dark green of the stones complementing the pale green of her dress, with the muted gold of the shoes matching the muted gold of the jewelry.

She'd nibbled on a bit of salad, but had largely forgotten to eat all day. She'd kept herself in a meditative state, enjoying each moment. Polishing her nails, taking a long jetted Epsom salts bath, arranging her hair, dallying with her makeup, thoughtfully getting dressed.

Calm all day long, her nerves never flared. She remained in peaceful contemplation. She didn't think about the evening. She gave the evening permission to unfold precisely as it meant to.

At five-thirty, she sat comfortably in the overstuffed chair, arms on the arm rests, waiting quietly for Gregory. Before long, the door bell rang. He was early, and she'd anticipated that.

When she opened the door, Gregory stood grinning hugely at her, holding a giant bundle of yellow roses and baby's breath. "For my favorite artist!"

"Oh, Gregory, they're beautiful. But, you shouldn't have!" She drank in their heady fragrance. "I want to take them with me. They're so appropriate for the opening."

"That's a good idea. I was going to get you red roses, because that's the stereotype. But then I thought about the meadowlark and the yellow-orange tones in *Freesia Bridge* and decided yellow would be a better color, as your work tends to subtler colors."

"Artist to the core, you are, dear friend."

"Oh! Alison!" He appeared tongue-tied for a moment, then recovered. "Well, let me look at you. *Wow!* You're stunning! Perfect, perfect, perfect," he noted, checking out the dress, and the emeralds. "And ... you're going barefoot," he added.

Alison laughed. "No. But, you'll have to endure my dispelling the overall effect while I throw on my Nikes to go down my stairs." She picked up the shoe box and opened it. "But for the show, I'm wearing these new shoes. Three-inch heels, which I almost never wear. I hope I don't kill my feet."

"Ah—but what a way to go, little feet! Are you ready?"

"Yes." Alison slipped on her Nikes, picked up her small green and gold beaded bag and the shoe box, and locked the door. Gregory held onto the roses, and, offering her his arm, they made their way to his car.

After they were seated he gave her another studied look. "You're glowing! I mean, you're practically glowing in the dark."

She laughed. "Yes. I'm known to do that when especially happy!"

"I wonder how far away I'll have to park," Gregory mused as they neared the gallery.

"I shall invoke the fairies to provide you with the space you've had the last couple times," Alison intoned.

But when they arrived at the gallery, the block was parked up solid both directions, as far as the eye could see. As Gregory started to moan, a car in the exact space in front of the gallery turned on its lights and pulled out.

"*Oh! Alison!*" Gregory whispered.

"*I know!*" she whispered back.

He silently parked while Alison slipped on her shoes. Then he came around and opened her door. "There's magic afoot," he said.

"I believe you." She handed him the roses, as he gave her his hand to stand.

"Whoa! You're tall!"

Alison giggled.

They walked to the gallery. Mr. Styikes stood in the doorway, watching their every move.

"I think Mr. Styikes is in cahoots with my fairies to clear the parking space."

"It seems probable."

Jen opened the door for them. "Thank you, Jen," Alison said, then turned to Mr. Styikes, surprised to see that she was now an inch taller than he. "Thank you for this evening, Mr. Styikes."

"No, no, thank you, Alison, dear. Beautiful yellow roses, a perfect complement to your work."

"Yes, Gregory has an eye for surroundings."

"Gregory, yes. Gregory. Good to see you." He shook his hand. "Jan, please be a dear and put these lovely flowers in an appropriate vase."

"Yes, Mr. Styikes." She took the roses and fled off into the nether reaches of the gallery.

He turned back to Alison. "It's early, but people will come soon. People always come early and stay late at my openings."

"I'm sure that's a good thing," Alison observed.

"I'm sure it is, too. They come early in case there's something they might want to buy and don't want to miss it. They come late because they had to do other things, but still, do not want to miss it."

As if on cue, several people came through the front door behind Alison. She turned to greet some of her current students who came together. Comfort in numbers, Alison thought.

"Hi!" Alison said, smiling.

"I think we're early," one of them said. "I think we're extremely early, but they insisted. They said they didn't want to have to look over other people's heads to see your work. So, I apologize for all of us that we're so early."

"No problem, I'm sure. Mr. Styikes was just saying that people always come early to his openings. Mr.

Styikes, these are a few of my students ....” She was about to introduce them all around when Jen called to her.

“Excuse me, I’ll be right back.” She went to Jan who held the roses in one hand and a clear glass vase in another. “Is this vase all right? It looks good to me, but he has, like, shelves of vases. I like this clear glass that doesn’t upstage the roses.”

“I agree with you. Good eye, Jan. Where’s Jen?”

“She’ll be here shortly. She has another part time job. For openings, she has to go home and get dressed up. She usually gets here right at seven.”

Alison nodded.

“I’ll put the roses at the front desk. Does that seem all right?”

“Perfect.”

Mr. Styikes called to her. She grinned at Jan and rejoined him. Gregory stood chatting with her students, classmates and pals of his.

Suddenly, everything was a whirl. Current and past students arrived, some of them apologizing for being late as they’d had to hike several blocks before finding a place to park, others arriving by city transportation. At the same time, limos pulled up, letting out elegantly dressed couples and groups. Some of the people Alison knew, while many of them she’d never met.

She hardly had time to wander about, standing quietly behind people to listen to them discuss her work, which she particularly liked to do. Yes, sometimes she had to endure a criticism, but that only improved her work when someone said something that was right on target.

But mostly she loved it when people saw things in her work that she herself had not seen. Whether she agreed or disagreed didn't matter to her nearly as much as seeing the work from a different perspective.

Mr. Styikes had provided a mountain of delectables in one of the side rooms, along with a variety of wines, which was rapidly depleting.

But the biggest surprise of the evening was watching her prints getting wrapped up and out the door, as well as little "Sold" stickers on more and more of her originals on the walls.

Thank goodness she'd had NFS placed on *Freesia Bridge*. She learned that Mr. Styikes, Jan, and Jen were receiving and making entries of offers on it.

A news team came, shot a bit of footage, took a snippet of comment from Mr. Styikes, herself, and a couple of her students. It was almost more than she could take in.

It was, in fact, *absolutely* more than she could take in!

Gregory, happily, kept entertained with the flow of students, for which she was grateful or she would feel like she was abandoning him. But no—every time she glanced at him, he was smiling and fully in his element.

He was more in *his* element, being in *her* element, than she was.

All so exciting and perfect. And yet, she would *still* prefer to be home, painting.

She'd not worn a watch, and Mr. Styikes cleverly did not have a clock on the wall. No, no, let people not think about time. Let them buy art!

She asked the man who was chatting her up, raving about her technique, what time he had. "Eight-thirty," he said. "Sill plenty of time for more people to come!" he grinned, having no idea that she truly was ready for the evening to be over.

"Thank you," she nodded, while someone else came up to chat with her. Eight-thirty. Much art sold, and a perfect evening.

People were so sweet. They wanted to know how she created this effect, or where she got that inspiration. It was all treasured by her. And exhausting. She thought she might try to step from the gallery into a back room with a closed door for a few moments, when she heard a familiar voice.

"Alison!"

She turned. There stood Sage.

Chapter 13
Sage

She couldn't have been more shocked if a zebra appeared in the doorway.

"Sage? Really? Is it really you? How ...?"

Sage rushed to her and gave her a big hug. "Yes, it's me. I sent you that message and then I thought, what's the matter with me? That was a terrible thing to do, because it probably completely disrupted your energy. And then I thought, *wait!* There's no reason in the world for me not to come up and see your show. There it was, clearly advertised on the website, and so I jumped on a plane and came!"

Still in a bit of shock, Alison could hardly think, let alone speak. "I ... I'm so glad you're here."

"Me too. Show me your work." She stopped and looked around. "Goodness, the place is packed!"

"Yes. It's been quite the event. But I'm ... I was trying to figure out a way I might escape for a few minutes, refresh and return as, Mr. Styikes, the gallery owner, said there's likely to be a big last minute crowd. And right now, I'm done."

"You'll be all right. I'm here, you can lean on me. You look fantastic."

"Thanks, Sage."

Mr. Styikes came up to them, "And who is this breath-taking young woman?"

This is my friend from Southern California who has nearly caused me to faint by making a completely surprise visit. Sage Elgin, this is Mr. Styikes, the owner of this beautiful gallery."

"Indeed, it *is* beautiful. And even more so graced with Alison's work. I was about to have her take me on a tour."

"Let us, then, embark," Mr. Styikes said, taking Sage by the elbow, and leading her back to the first painting in the show. Alison tagged along, but heard little of the banter that passed between them.

Gregory, still engrossed in chat with her various students, caught her eye and raised an eyebrow, mouthing, "who?"

"Sage," she silently mouthed in return.

"*Wow!*" he said aloud, disrupting the conversational flow in his little group.

She watched as he excused himself and came over to her, still tagging along behind Mr. Styikes and Sage. "You didn't tell me about this," he said quietly.

"That would be because I didn't know."

Sage, hearing Alison talk, turned to face Gregory. "I think you must be Gregory." She extended her hand. "I'm Sage."

"How do you know my name?"

"Alison has said wonderful things about you."

"She has, has she?"

"Umm-hum." Sage turned to Alison. "Your work, it's … it's … what's the best word? It touches me. It's not only beautiful, there's an emotional undercurrent that I feel from every one of them … I love it. And I'm becoming more and more disappointed—I mean, happy for you of course,—but disappointed to see SOLD on practically everything. I fear there will be nothing left for me to buy."

Alison chuckled. "Well, fortunately, you know the artist quite well, so—all is not lost."

Sage sighed a great sigh. "Thank goodness!"

Jan came up to Mr. Styikes cautiously, but Alison knew she would not approach him if it wasn't important.

"There seems to be a bit of a disagreement over here," she said quietly."

"Oh, dear, the kids will on occasion get into a rumble. Carry on, I shall return."

"So tell me, Gregory, what sort of an art teacher is Alison? I will preface your comments with my own, namely that she is an amazing life skills teacher."

"She's an amazing art teacher, as well. Enough direction to get you in motion, enough freedom to discover your genius."

"Perfect. That describes her perfectly."

Alison felt shy. "I think I ought to be somewhere else, so you two can carry on this conversation that you're having as though I'm not here, with me actually not here."

Sage laughed, putting her arm around Alison. "Please absorb the accolades you've earned. But, perhaps, Gregory, we might not speak of her in the third person."

"Perhaps."

"Now, suddenly, I feel done," Alison said. "All has gone perfectly. And now, all I want is have the two of you over to my place, with the three of us sitting cozily in front of the fire. But *first*, kicking of these darn shoes. Tall is great. Pain is not."

"I thought you seemed taller," Sage acknowledged. "Of course me, up here at over six feet in heels, lots of people are ... shorter. Never mind that, I love the sound of your plan. But I must finish my tour of your work, in this so-perfect setting."

"Yes. Let us finish our circuit. I'll tag along, but perhaps, Gregory, you would pick up where Mr. Styikes left off with the chat. I'm not up to describing my work any more."

"Happily," Gregory beamed.

Alison followed quietly as the three of them made their circuit around the gallery. They picked up the thread of their conversation as if she was not there. It suited her perfectly.

They finally came around the last wall where *Freesia Bridge* hung.

"*Oh, Alison!*" Sage exclaimed. "You added the freesia bridge since Monday?"

"I did it on Tuesday, yes. I'd done the cottonwood and meadowlark, I'd done the little farmstead. But for months I couldn't figure out how to tie the two components together, as you heard me say before. Then, the freesia bridge appeared."

"Brilliant! Simply brilliant, Alison. NFS. Not for sale?"

"Not until I get some prints made. From what Mr. Styikes says, it has sold more than once tonight, with various offers."

"I can understand that." Sage stepped back and studied the painting quietly. "Awesome. If the painting has a wait list, I can't do much about that. But I do want a print, pretty, pretty please."

"But of course. I'd be honored. After all, I would not have had the inspiration if you hadn't taken me to the arboretum."

Sage, who'd looked a bit sad and disappointed, perked up considerably. "That's true! I'm so glad to have had a part in this exquisite piece."

"I'm glad you did too!" Alison agreed. Then, without segue asked, "What time is it?"

Gregory looked at his watch. "Just this minute, nine p.m."

"Oh, yay, soon this great joy will be over."

Sage and Gregory chuckled, while at that moment, a boisterous crowd came through the front door. It sounded to Alison like hundreds of people, and her face showed her disappointment.

"This, too, shall pass," Gregory affirmed.

Resigned, Alison nodded. "I must go be friendly. You know those truculent artists Mr. Styikes referred to last night? I think I'll become one."

Gregory turned to Sage, "No she won't," they said in unison. They followed her to the front door.

There Alison met a group of expensively dressed, but fairly inebriated people. Mr. Styikes, right behind of her, passed her to extend his gracious welcome.

"Welcome to Styikes' Gallery. I'm Mr. Styikes. Let me show you around our opening, this evening. This is the artist, Alison Williamson."

"Wow! You're hot," one of the noisy crowd exclaimed. The whole group, guffawed.

"You're supposed to say the artist's work is hot, not that the artist is hot," one of the women fairly bellowed.

"I'd like to see her work! Will you come and work for me," the obnoxious man continued.

Alison watched as the expression on Mr. Styikes face changed from congenial to ... something else entirely. The inappropriate behavior of these rabble-rousers offended her, but her curiosity how he'd handle the situation set aside her irritation.

The tone of Mr. Styikes voice changed in tenor, affirming he'd not tolerate continued inappropriate behavior. "Again, you are all welcome to my private establishment. But proper decorum is required. You will not be addressing any of my artists in the familiar, unless, of course, you're a member of her family. Are you related to Ms. Williamson?

The lead rabble rouser was stymied for a clever retort—for obvious reasons.

"Tone it down, Mark, or he'll send us out," one of the other women said. "My sister takes a class from Ms. Williamson and I want to see her work."

"All right. I'll try to behave myself."

Alison couldn't see the woman who spoke, but she wanted to make the best of the situation by being friendly with the one person who appeared sane in the group.

"Who's your sister?"

The woman made her way through the group. "Hi, Ms. Williamson. Marcy Marshall, and I'm Marie. She's said wonderful things about you, and I've been, I have to tell you, quite surprised at some of the work she's produced in your class. I didn't know she had it in her."

Alison smiled warmly. "Oh, yes, Marcy. She has quite a talent, a wonderful raw talent. She was here earlier this evening with a couple of her classmates."

"Maybe I'll have to take your class and see if I have any raw talent."

"That would be lovely." Alison drew the tiny woman into the gallery. "Please, come in and take a look at my work."

"Raw talent, yeah, likely story," Mark, the rabble-rouser wisecracked.

"Be nice!" one of the other women advised.

Alison had a deep, deep sensation that Mark was about to escalate his disagreeable behavior, and had an inclination to move herself, and Marie, if possible, away from the offender. "I think you might like this painting I worked on in class when Marcy was there." She moved another twelve feet from the fulmination.

"Oh yes!" Marie exclaimed, "I recognize it. Her description was quite accurate."

Alison couldn't help but give her attention to the trouble brewing. She glanced over at Gregory, still chatting with Sage. They had wandered back to revisit some of the other paintings.

He caught her eye. A scowl on her face, she made a small nod to the front door. Did she feel guilty sending her friend into the fray? Not one bit as he was a modest—but dangerous—kung fu master. She'd never needed this talent of his, but it came into play at this moment.

He put his hand on Sage's elbow and excused himself graciously, then moved to the front of the gallery.

Mr. Styikes was still holding the fort, but Gregory shifted the energy. Alison found it fascinating how male animals—*including humans!*—always seemed to get it when one of their species could truly do them harm.

She heard the little bell over the door tinkle and felt despair that yet more people were coming into the gallery, even this long after the publicized end of the opening.

"Thank you all for coming to the opening," Mr. Styikes said over the general hubbub. "Miss Williamson and I are grateful for your interest, but the opening is now over. Please return tomorrow during our regular hours. Thank you!"

Marie looked around nervously. "Should I leave?"

"Only if one of the people in that group is your ride."

"No. I drove myself. I don't actually know them. They're an art meetup, and I've gone to a couple openings with the group. But, no, I'm happy to say I'm not dependent on them. And probably won't join them again after this embarrassing event."

"Not to worry, dear. Please take your time and enjoy my work. People who are here for the right reason are invited to linger." Alison looked over her shoulder at the disarray of the group leaving. Someone was making a all-out effort to go against traffic to come into the gallery. Gregory and Mr. Styikes continued to energetically force the offending group to leave, in the quietest, most civilized, manner.

But one person doggedly forged his way into the gallery against the tide. Soon, he succeeded. Soon only Mr. Styikes, Gregory, and this third forceful person were the only people at the door.

Yes, it must be old-home night, Alison thought, because there between them stood Anthony.

Chapter 14
A Proposal

Alison looked over at Sage, who looked, in shock, at Anthony. She caught Sage's look, but still she had to ask. "Did you know he was coming?"

"No, I didn't."

Sage took in Alison's expression, then hurried toward Anthony. "Anthony! What a surprise. I can't believe you're here!"

His look of astonishment at seeing Sage matched hers at seeing him. "*Nor I, you!*" he exclaimed.

Mr. Styikes and Gregory relaxed their position around Anthony, as Sage came to his side. "My goodness, you almost missed the opening, altogether. Mr. Styikes, Gregory, this is my friend and neighbor, Anthony Williamson."

Anthony first extended his hand to Mr. Styikes, "Very pleased to meet ...."

"Williamson, Alison's last name?" Mr. Styikes repeated.

"Yes. Alison's ex, I believe, if I'm not mistaken," Gregory offered.

"Oh! I see," Mr. Styikes said sounding confused, shaking Anthony's hand.

Alison's ex? Alison thought, reeling from the sound of it. Strangely enough, she'd never heard that phrase. When she left Anthony, she moved to San Francisco and told almost no one about her past. Except Gregory. And now he said, what anyone would say.

Anthony turned to Gregory, and extended his hand, which Alison saw Gregory take most unenthusiastically. Meanwhile, Mr. Styikes gave Alison a look that said, "I'll throw him out if you want me to."

Reluctantly, she joined the little group. "I'm flattered, Anthony, that you want to see my work. But, why didn't you tell me you planned on coming?"

Anthony moved away from Mr. Styikes and Gregory. "I decided, on a whim, to come today. I did a search of your name and 'art openings in San Francisco' and up it popped. I intended to take a peek at your work, if some of the show was online. But then I decided to jump on a plane and see it live and in person And to see you, Alison, live and in all your stunning glory. You're breathtaking."

"Thank you, Anthony," Alison said, the epitome of politeness.

"So off I dashed to the airport, only to discover the flight was full and over-booked. I had to wait for the next flight, and almost missed your opening altogether."

"My goodness, that was quite persistent of you."

"It was. And then," he chuckled, "I almost got thrown out before I came in, with that rowdy group."

"So you almost were. But again you persisted."

"Yes. And here I am. I know, Alison, your opening is over at nine." He turned to Mr. Styikes, "But is it all right if I appreciate Alison't art, Mr. Styikes?"

"I don't mind if Alison doesn't mind. There are still others here, and still a bit of food and wine."

"I'm fine—if a bit in shock—that he's here." Alison tried to ignore the storm that gathered on Gregory's brow. It made her sad. He'd been so happy all evening, and he'd worked so hard to help her get to and through this evening. There was probably no one he'd rather less see than Anthony.

"Let's take a quick tour, Anthony, while not keeping Mr. Styikes and his employees and Gregory too long. They've all worked so hard to put together this beautiful show, and everyone is tired."

Marie, who'd stood to the side watching the drama made her way to the door. "I will come back tomorrow, Alison, to take in the rest of your beautiful work. It's been lovely meeting you."

"It's been lovely meeting you, too, Marie. And I hope to see you in class."

"I plan on it. Bye!" She made her way through the little knot of people at the door.

"I'll likely do the same, come back tomorrow to give each piece studied appreciation. But thank you, Mr. Styikes, for letting me look at Alison's work, with her present," Anthony said.

"Of course," Mr. Styikes said.

Anthony nodded his gratitude and moved to the first painting.

Nearly overwhelmed with a cascade of feelings, Alison joined him, with Sage tagging along.

"Hmmm," Anthony said, hand to chin, studying the painting. "Lovely." He moved to the next one. "Oh, this is delightful. It feels rather familiar." He moved closer to read the title. "In the woods. Of course! The birches at the stream, where we were Sunday, on our ride! Most eloquently captured, Alison. Truly beautiful work. 'Sold,' Ah, what a pity! Good for you, but sad for me."

Alison stepped back to study her own painting. She hadn't realized before that it was, in fact, a nearly precise rendering of the woods where she and Sage had felt the fairies, only a few days before, but she'd painted the work over a year before. The subconscious *would* take over when given freedom, she thought. And effective artistic creating was most assuredly giving the subconscious freedom.

Anthony moved to the third painting. At this rate, they'd be here all night, watching Anthony make little comments. Strangely, it was surprisingly difficult to watch him study her work. She didn't know why, and she didn't want to think about it.

She still wanted, more than anything, to be in her cozy home, in a loose, flowing caftan, sipping wine with Gregory and Sage. And *Gregory and Sage only*, around a lit fireplace.

That's what she wanted. She couldn't hold another piece of information right now, while the appearance of Anthony was quite a bit more than 'a piece of information.' It was a-lot-and-too-much-information.

Anthony moved to the third painting, then noticed that Alison was no longer accompanying him. "Alison? Oh my, you look tired. I'm a clod. Like your little friend who had the decency to say she would come back tomorrow to study the show, I, too, will do the same."

Alison tried not to make her sigh of relief visible.

"I look forward to it," Mr. Styikes said. "I love the day after a successful opening, when the people who return really want to appreciate the work. I believe tomorrow will be a pretty busy day."

"But, Alison, might I take a look at the painting that you said was made complete by the freesias?"

"Of course," Alison said graciously. "It's the last painting in the show." She took him around the wall to *Freesia Bridge*.

Anthony, smiling, looked at the painting. Then the smile faded from his face. "How ... Alison, how did you do this? How did you ... this is an image ...." He stepped back from the painting, and bit his lip. "How could you do this?" he whispered.

"What, Anthony, what are you saying?"

"This is a picture from my childhood. My young childhood, when I was about nine. You don't know this. That summer I went to live with my grandparents. They had a little farm in Kansas. This image is straight out of my memories from that summer.

"One summer day, I was feeling so sad I missed my parents too much. I went for a walk, and came to a stand of gigantic, tall, cottonwoods, and there, precisely like you have painted, I saw a meadowlark, on a low branch, right in front of my eyes. *Just like this*, I've carried the picture in my mind and heart all these years, but never shared it with anyone. No. One. Not even you.

"I sat on the ground and listened to that beautiful, haunting song, watching the little bird, all alone, and yet so happy. So happy to simply be alive and singing. It changed me. Deep inside. That little bird taught me that I could find happiness. I could find my song, even when alone."

"I walked back to their farmhouse and crossed the little flower-strewn bridge over the pond. There were fragrant flowers everywhere, in a riot of colors. I remember smelling the sweet flowers and still hearing the meadowlark's sweet song.

"I'd been vey seriously contemplating running away from that farm and trying to find my way back home. Without a clue, of course, how to do it. Not because my grandparents were anything other loving. But I didn't want to be there. Until that moment. That changed my life.

"That's why I built the mansion on acreage, in honor of that deep, internal, private moment in my childhood, when I decided to stay at their farm."

Anthony turned to Alison, bemused. "I ... how did you do this?"

Stunned almost to stillness, Alison whispered, "I don't know, Anthony." She paused. What could she say but the truth? "I started this painting months ago. But it refused to come together. Something was missing. Then, the illusion of the stem of freesias the other day, when I bent down to look at them closely, it visually appeared to be overarching the little duck pond, in the distance. And ..." she hesitated. She wanted to tell him about how he came into view at that exact moment, looking undecided about crossing the freesia bridge. But it was too much.

It was all just a bit too much.

"And, I felt certain that the 'snapshot' my mind took in that moment would complete the image."

"Yes," Anthony agreed solemnly, clearly shaken up. He stepped close to it. "Not for sale?" He turned to look at her.

"I've not had a chance to make prints. I believe several have been pre-sold. Also, Mr. Styikes told me there have been several offers on the original."

"Of course." Anthony nodded. "Despite the fact that it is my own, extremely personal picture, it would resonate with anyone with a heart. It's ... inspired." Anthony's voice quavered.

Alison had only seen him in this crush of emotional upheaval twice in her life. When his mother died, and when she told him she was leaving him.

And this painting, *her* painting, brought all of that boiling up in him. She hadn't been married to him for twenty years without knowing, feeling, sensing his emotions.

"Thank you, Anthony. I ... I'll leave you alone for a few moments with *Freesia Bridge*. I need to have a chat with Mr. Styikes."

"All right," Anthony said simply, not taking his eyes from the painting.

Alison returned to the little group that had gathered at the front desk, Mr. Styikes, Jan, Jen, Gregory and Sage, who had left Alison and Anthony to their privacy.

"Thank you for being so patient. I've left him with the painting for a few moments. But, Mr. Styikes, what must we attend to yet tonight?"

"Nothing, my dear. The only thing that this moment needs is my ritual closing glass of bubbly for a job exceedingly well done, and it would give me great pleasure if Sage and Anthony joined us."

"Thank you, that is ever so kind," Anthony said, coming up to them. "And my profound apologies for crashing the opening, I was so focused, especially after not getting on the flight I'd intended. I cannot express my gratitude when the driver pulled up to the gallery, and I saw a large group of people milling about.

"Of course, I had no way of knowing they were misbehaving and unwelcome, and you were trying to get them out!" He chuckled.

Mr. Styikes led the way to his inner sanctum, where the bottle of champagne in a bucket of ice awaited them.

"I'll get a couple more glasses," Jan said, and scurried off, soon returning with two more of the elegant champagne flutes. Mr. Styikes popped the cork and filled glasses, handing them, one by one to each person present. Then he held his glass aloft. "No big declaration. Simply, job well done, everyone, thank you, and thank you Alison's muse, without whom we would not be here tonight."

"Truer words were never spoken," Alison agreed, as they clinked glasses. "Whatever art I have comes entirely from my Muse."

*　　*

Soon they were all standing on the other side of the front door, wishing one another a good night, while Mr. Styikes locked the gallery up tight.

Alison waved to Jan, Jen, and Mr. Styikes as they went off to the parking structure where Mr. Styikes kept his car—he always took Jan and Jen home when they stayed particularly late, as they both, otherwise, depended on public transportation.

Gregory, Sage, Anthony, and Alison stayed in a slightly uneasy knot, no one knowing quite what to do.

"Will you stay in my humble little guest room tonight, Sage?"

"With delight!" Sage replied.

"Excellent. Why don't the two of you get in the car, it's a bit chilly, while I chat with Anthony for a few moments."

"All right," Gregory said quietly. "Come on Sage, let's stay warm."

Alison watched the two of them get into Gregory's car, then she turned to face the gallery. She couldn't help her curiosity. What did her work look like from the night sidewalk? It was beautiful! Mr. Styikes' impeccable sense of light and dark and balance all came to play on her work in the gallery's spotlights in the night.

No one who took a night stroll would be able to resist standing here, gazing at her charming, pulling-at-heart-strings paintings. She realized she would come down here in the night herself while her show was up to watch people enjoy her work.

Oh dear, the yellow roses! She'd meant to take them with her. But no, they were better here through tomorrow.

Anthony remained silent, understanding her contemplation.

She finally turned to him. "I ... I can't take any more input right at this moment, Anthony. I had a plan to have Gregory over after the opening, and I would kick my shoe off, light the fire, drink dessert wine, and the two of us revel in the success. Assuming it was one. Which it was. Then Sage appears. That's lovely, and I still have a plan of going home, kicking my shoes off, getting into a soft, over-sized caftan, lighting the fire, drinking dessert wine, and reveling in the moment with Gregory and Sage. I'm equally comfortable with both of them.

"But, candidly, Anthony, I'm *not* comfortable with you. And although I feel boorish to not invite you too, you have come uninvited, and, I'm sorry, but I'm not inviting you to join us."

Anthony's brow furrowed. "You ... you sound angry."

"No, not quite angry. But ... almost. This feels manipulative. I have zero tolerance for manipulative behavior. You'll have to find your own way tonight. Call a Lyft, have them take you to a hotel."

"All right, Alison, I will do that. You're right about my behavior being inappropriate. But all I wanted all last weekend was a chance to simply talk with you for a couple hours." Anthony sighed, looking weary. "I still hope that's not too much to ask. May I not have a couple hours of your time?"

What he said was true, and she had already had the thought that she'd effectively blocked him from talking to her the entire time she was in Orange County.

"I will talk with you, Anthony. Tomorrow. If you really are coming here to look at the rest of my work, I'll meet you here. I have to discuss with Mr. Styikes how many prints are on order, and I want to take those lovely yellow roses Gregory gave me home with me."

"Yellow roses," Anthony observed. "Friendship...."

"He said they represent his feeling that yellow roses complement the soft hues that dominate my work. But, anyway, yes, I'll talk with you."

"What time?"

"I want to sleep until I'm done sleeping, and then I want to chat with Sage without feeling rushed. The gallery closes at six tomorrow, so, I'd say I'll be here around four."

"Four. All right. That's good. Goodnight, Alison." He gave her a nearly arm's reach hug. "Beautiful work, Ali-girl. I'm so proud of you," he whispered.

Without a word, she turned and hurried to Gregory's car. Anthony had not called her that private endearment in *years*. It struck her to her heart. She got in the car and Gregory started to pull out.

"Just a moment," she said. She looked at Anthony, who had turned away from the car, as if he couldn't stand to see it leave. In that moment she saw the little boy, gathering his courage inspired by the meadowlark that sang, despite being alone.

She could resist him when he was strong. But this ... she felt her resolve weaken.

"All right, take me home, my friend. I need to kick my shoes off!"

"Yeah, and speaking of which, get those Nikes on!"

"Right. Oh, thank goodness I brought them. I am done with these shoes, beautiful though may be, they are *devices of torture!*"

She kicked her shoes off, and slipped on the *devices of comfort.*

Soon she was in her living room, having changed into the longed-for caftan, barefoot, lighting the fire. Then she lit incense while Gregory brought out the two bottles of wines and the dessert wine purchased for the occasion.

Yet another time, she thought, Gregory was the best of friends. She'd never learned much about wines. But Gregory was an amateur connoisseur, and she left the final decisions of the "celebratory beverages" at the winery up to him.

She'd already taken Sage upstairs to the charming little guest room to let her get comfortable. Sage came down now in a pale yellow lounge outfit, and curled up in the corner of the sofa. With ceremony, Gregory brought the tray of wines and glasses to the coffee table.

Alison matched Sage by curling up in the overstuffed chair by the fireplace.

"What is everyone's pleasure?"

"You know mine," Alison said. "Dessert wine, without apology."

"And you, Sage?"

"The same. Sweets to the sweet."

"True, true," Gregory agreed, pouring the concoction into two small snifters and, with exaggerated gestures, offered them to his patrons.

"For myself, dear Alison, do you mind if I uncork the red?"

"Not in the least, my friend. More sweet wine for us!"

Soon Gregory held a glass of deep red wine up in the evocative firelight. "To a wildly successful opening, and a fabulously talented artist."

"So true!" Sage agreed. "To our beloved Alison. May her fingers always be stained with paint."

"Good one, Sage!" Gregory grinned broadly. "I feel like this is a personal triumph, if I may!"

"You may, *you must!*" Alison exclaimed. "The success of this show has your energy all over it, from kindness, to inspiration, to encouragement, to transportation, to feeding me, to hard, grunt labor. It's absolutely as much your show as mine."

Gregory showed his usual discomfort to broad compliments, where he sat in the shadowed far corner of the sofa.

"He's a shy boy, is he not?" Sage observed.

"He's an immensely shy boy," Alison agreed.

"Yes, I *am* shy." He leaned forward into the firelight. "But I'm not too shy to say that I am profoundly grateful that you didn't invite Anthony to be here with us in this moment."

"Oh! On another hand, he can really speak his mind," Sage observed, raising her eyebrows.

"Also quite true. Quite true."Alison nodded, although, frankly surprised by Gregory's direct comment. And now, doubly grateful that she'd not invited Anthony.

They fell into the hypnotic occupation of silent fire watching for a few moments.

"I told him that I felt utterly comfortable with the two of you, and looked ardently forward to *this* moment. But that he made me uncomfortable, and I would not invite him to share this special moment. He came uninvited, and it felt manipulative. It made me a little bit angry."

"But you don't feel that way about me?" Sage asked.

"Of course not. Never."

"Well, whatever the reasoning or conversation, I'm still glad he's gone," Gregory said softly.

"Not ... gone. Just, not ... here. I agreed to meet with him tomorrow, late in the afternoon. I have to talk with Mr. Styikes about how many and which prints he has pre-sold and if I have to print more, and, too, as beautiful as they are there, and I'm happy to leave them there tomorrow for the first full day of my show, I want to bring my beautiful roses home."

"I wondered about that," Gregory said. "But … so … you've agreed to meet with Anthony?"

"I have. I see now that the time I was down there last week, he'd tried, oh so appropriately, to simply have a talk with me. And I avoided it, I got around it. I shamelessly used Sage as a foil. But he asked politely tonight, and, yes, he deserves to be heard."

"What do you think he's going to say?"

"I truly do not know." Alison paused. "No, I don't know."

"Are you curious?" Gregory pressed.

"Of course." She looked at Sage. "You're mysteriously quiet."

"Just … listening." They exchanged a glance, and Alison knew that Sage had brought the strange little locked journal with her, and, along with coming to see her show, sharing the information it contained was equally important.

Perhaps more important.

The three of them shared another glass of warmth, then Sage took her leave. "I'm sorry if I'm a party poop, but I'm falling asleep, right here. That adorable little bed upstairs is calling and calling to me. I don't know how you're staying awake, Alison, after this day!"

"Ah, you must answer the call of the little bed. I had a calm, lazy day, puttering around. Now unwound, I'm feeling a bit of an adrenaline rush. Unlike you, I didn't have to get packed, drive to the airport, fly to another city, and get transportation to a place I've never been.

"Sleep well, Sage, and I'll see you ... whenever you please to come down."

"Sounds perfect." Sage stood and Gregory jumped up. "Not necessary! Please, sit down."

"No. I want to give you a hug."

"Oh, well, that's a different matter, altogether. Hug, please!"

Alison beamed at her two dear friends becoming friends. "I'm so brilliant, having the two of you meet!"

They laughed as Sage went around the corner and up the stairs.

Gregory sat back down, but then, got up and, taking a cushion from the sofa, plopped it in front of the fire by Alison's chair. He sat on the cushion facing the fire, leaning against the coffee table.

"Cozy," Alison noted.

"Very," Gregory agreed. "Look, Alison, if Anthony is going to talk with you tomorrow, I must talk with you tonight."

"No. you must not."

"No, I must."

Alison stopped sparring, a twinge of anxiety growing in her chest.

"He is going to ask you to come back to him...."

"I don't know that. And you can't know that."

"Oh, yes, I do know. Do you think I didn't watch him carefully? Do you think I don't get what's going on?"

"What's going on?"

"Dear, please follow along in your hymnal. As just recited, he's going to ask you to come back to him."

"Oh, I see. And we could go around on the same chorus again—but I won't."

"Good, because, this is … this is difficult for me, and I've never been here before. Well, not exactly true. I was here when I was nine."

"Where, exactly?"

"Asking a girl to marry me."

"You asked a girl to marry you when you were nine?"

"*Awk!* We're getting derailed, but yes."

"What did she say?"

"She said yes."

"Then what happened?"

"Her family moved away less than a month later."

"Oh! Her father did no approve of your two kingdoms uniting."

"In the vernacular, ahm, I suppose that might be true. Although I doubt he knew of the proposal."

"Do you think you'd still be married had it come to pass?"

"Knowing me, I'd say, yes. And, thus, neither you nor I would not be going through this difficult moment."

"Sad. Sad story, Gregory."

"Well, time heals most wounds."

"*All* wounds," Alison corrected.

"No. I don't think so. But, Alison, there's a proposal here, between us. I'm not on a knee, but I am down on the floor at your feet … if you weren't sitting on them. I'll get on one knee, if it'll make a difference."

Alison watched the fire dance across Gregory's face as he looked into it, not at her, because, as had been acknowledge, he was painfully shy.

But he was also amazing. Truly, deeply, kind, intelligent, talented, protective. And attractive.

But, still, no. Not because she didn't love him. She did. Dearly and completely. Not because she wouldn't be happy, she probably would be, but she suspected she'd not be as happy as she was now, so much in love with her independent life. Even though much of it had to do with him. The important point was—he was not there all the time.

That was the important piece. One had to think about someone being there *All. The. Time.* Tricky territory.

"You are quiet too long," Gregory said softly.

"Honorably weighing what you said, Gregory."

"All right." He remained silent.

"Here we go. I do love you, basically, unconditionally. You're kind, intelligent, talented, protective, physically attractive. We have great times, we laugh, share our talents, talk about deep subjects, fix the world—if only it would listen to us. And that is all so perfect. I don't want it to change.

"But I can't ... I can't make a picture of changing what we have into the stuff of marriage, so much of which is challenging and difficult. I want our time together to always be as wonderful as it has always been.

"And, marriage, I say again, would destroy it."

"But ... what if it wouldn't? What if everything that's wonderful was simply much more wonderful?"

"It wouldn't be."

"How can you know?"

"I know because ... because I simply do not feel 'that way' about you, my dearest Gregory. And if I haven't in the years we've known each other, it's not going to materialize.

"I know that people can surprise themselves, and be different from who they thought they were. But other thoughts, things ... cannot be changed."

She found herself beginning to say, "And I could only ever felt that way about Anthony, but stopped herself. Two thoughts. First of all, it would be even *more* hurtful to Gregory.

And secondly, *What!?!* She *had* only ever felt that way about Anthony–all right.

But *could* only ever feel that way about Anthony, and no one else?

What a conundrum. If she could only feel "that way"–romantically intimate—with Anthony, but could not feel "that way" with him because of his betrayal and immorality, then it followed that she would never again experience romantic love.

This thought needed more thinking. She hadn't looked this hard at that aspect of her feelings, because she hadn't been faced with it. Now, suddenly the stars, *or whatever*, had aligned to force her to look at the thought repeatedly in the space of a few days.

Gregory remained silent during these strange, philosophical thoughts. She looked down at him. He appeared to be deep within the realm of self-reflection, as well.

"Well, I guess," he finally said, "it's my own fault for not bringing it up before, so I wouldn't have wasted time with romantic notions. And I guess I have to sort out for myself how I feel about our relationship, now that you've made it so clear where it's *not* going, and will never go."

Oh dear, Alison found herself thinking, I'm going to lose my best friend.

"And I guess," he continued, "that, I too, have to evaluate the relationship as it is, and, at least superficially, agree that it's sort of perfect. All friendship, without the emotional and financial stresses of a marriage."

"Yes," Alison agreed. "Let's, neither one of us make decrees that are damaging to the relationship we have."

"Other than the decree you made, 'I could never feel that way about you.'"

"Oh, ouch, that sounds terrible when one hears it back."

"Hmmm…wasn't beauteous the first time, either."

"I'm sorry, my friend." She reached down and tousled his hair—something she had never done! "You are my best friend, you know."

He looked up at her, surprised. "Really!? What about … what about Sage?"

"Also a best friend. But she's a generation younger, and it's more of an aunt-niece relationship. But still, quite precious and pleasant."

"Yes. Aunt-niece, I see that. She slightly defers to you. You're slightly solicitous with her."

"*Sooo* perceptive," Alison exclaimed.

"What about Karen?"

"Yes, Karen. A special friend. We share a lot of laughs, and she takes excellent care of Miss Prissy, there, curled up sleeping." She pointed to the cat, who had wandered in a short while before. "Karen is a wonderful friend. And I have other friends, who make my life rich and full. But you, Gregory, are *my best friend*. I feel closest to you.

"We have the same sense of humor, we have utterly similar interests, we share our love of art, and going to art museums, and having talks that are really boring to others, but utterly fascinating to us."

"All right," Gregory finally pulled his gaze from the fire and looked up a her. "I'm a tiny bit placated. In this slightly better frame of mind, I believe I shall take my leave, with all I must contemplate." He stood up and stretched. "In any event, if I only ask this question once every few decades, I should, hopefully, keep myself from appearing too much the fool."

"You are none the fool. And, anyway, the first time, you were told yes."

"True. I've not looked at it quite that way." He helped her to her feet, gave her a hug and headed for the door. "All and all," he said, slipping on his shoes, "a spectacularly memorable day."

"A spectacularly memorable day," Alison agreed as he opened the door and stepped out into the night. "See you in class if not before."

He jaunted down the stairs. "See you in class."

She put away the wine, checked on the embers in the fireplace, picked up puss-cat and took the two of them to bed.

Chapter 15
The Mysterious Journal

When Alison woke up the next morning, she luxuriated for a few moments, basking in the feeling of a job well done, and nothing had to be done today.

Oh, wait, except for the uncomfortable bit about talking with Anthony. "Growl," she said, getting out of bed. "Don't want to do it."

She took a shower, slipped on a pair of jeans and a sweatshirt and went out to make something that resembled breakfast for herself and Sage. Except Sage was already in the kitchen, whipping up a fruit smoothie, with the teapot on.

"I was waiting for signs of life before whipping the fruit together. Good nutrition, young woman, that's what you need," Sage greeted cheerily.

"No argument, and I'm starving. I'm delighted that you've taken the initiative. You're hired!"

She sat at the breakfast bar, watching Sage put the finishing touches to smoothie and tea.

"How long did you two chat last night?" Sage asked.

"Oh, I think it was about one a.m. when Miss Prissy and I crawled into bed." She wanted to tell Sage about Gregory's proposal, because, well just because. But then, since she'd told him no, she realized that it had to remain between the two of them.

So, of course, Sage asked, "What did you talk about?"

"Oh," Alison answered evasively, "You know, the opening, the success of the opening. The drama during the opening."

"Nothing about Anthony."

"Sure. Of course. Talk about Anthony."

"And?"

"And, well, not surprisingly, he's not a fan of Anthony's. I've really not talked about Anthony much, but Gregory knows I was well and truly hurt, as is generally the case with divorces.

"But let's not talk of these dreary things of the past. Let us revel in your present, with Michael. Let us consider if we're going to do anything today, or simply sit around like a pair of frogs on lily pads, chatting all day until I must go to the gallery."

Sage giggled. "Oh, please, I much prefer the second option. I want to be a frog on a lily pad. Where's my lily pad?"

"I do believe you're sitting on it."

"Oh. Ah, *hmmm*, I shall refrain from making a comment about that ... comment. I shall sit here contentedly on my 'lily pad' drinking my tea, enjoying my fruit." She sipped her tea. "But, you know, Alison...."

"Yes, I suppose I do. The mysterious, tiny, locked, journal. That you say your aunt wrote in and then hid away."

"Oh the mark, Alison."

"I think I dread it. I ... I don't want to revisit that time. I don't want to see Victoria's handwriting.I don't want to read or hear any more of her lies. I know, Sage, you want to defend her. You don't want to hear me speak badly about her. I've always done my best to keep my thoughts to myself. But now you're dragging me, kicking and screaming, rather much, and in my own home, to a place I don't want to go.

"I suppose I could flatly refuse to look at it, and somewhat tyrannically insist that you never bring it up again. But ... against every fibre of my being, I am going to let you share with me this, this, whatever you think it is, that's so important, that it risks significantly upsetting me."

"Oh, dear ...." Sage said, softly, alarmed. "Oh, dear. Am I doing a wrong thing? Am I getting up in your business and I have no business being there? Now I'm torn. I thought it extremely important for you to see this weird confession. But there it is. And, you, you've done a startlingly good job of keeping these intensely strong opinions about Aunt Victoria to yourself.

"Oh, Alison!" Sage started to cry.

Alison couldn't bear to see "her" precious girl crying, and she completely melted. "It's all right, Sage. It's all right. We'll look at Victoria's little confession book. And I'll just be adult about it. I'm ... I've had the most roller-coaster week in many years, and I'm simply not even-tempered." She patted Sage on the back soothingly.

"It's all right, my girl. Don't cry, you'll make your lovely fruit drink too salty."

Sage cracked a small smile. "Don't make me laugh, I'm busy being sad."

At this, Alison laughed out loud. "Now, that's a bumper sticker for the depressed! I think we could make a fortune off of it. All righty now, let's finish our refreshing, healthy, lovely breakfast, and we'll pore over this mysterious journal."

Thy finished their breakfast, then Sage ran up to her room and brought down the little locked journal. Alison turned on the light that hung over the sofa, while Sage looked up at her, then back to the journal, unlocking it. She had put a little sticky bookmark near the middle of the book. Without saying anything, she opened the book to that page and handed it to Alison.

Breathing deeply, Alison began to read ... it appeared to be in the middle of an entry, but she directly understood why Sage felt it relevant.

Well, Journal, little confession Journal, that some part of me insists on writing in, recording things I don't want anyone to know. And yet, I must write them out. Why? Guilt? Pah! I have not time for guilt! Life is short, and the spoils go to she who does not look back.

But, all right, Journal, since you insist. Here is one of my big secrets. Anthony and I have never "consummated" our—whatever this is. Relationship. There now. Does that take care of this nagging thing in my mind? Where it comes from, I do not know.

Men. They're so ... irritating. Look, Journal, I've never cared to be close to anyone. I don't know why. I know that I have an incredible power over men, for some reason. Beauty. Oh sure, yes. That's hypnotic for men. Being unavailable seems to drive them to try to make a part of me that does not exist, blossom. This some of them have as much as said.

That's why I stayed married to that poor sap all his life. He wasn't one-tenth as intelligent as me, but he remained weirdly besotted with me his whole life, without us ever being close. He lived a life of illusion, based on my looks.

But Anthony ... a different story. Brilliant and good-looking. A conquest. A game. I wanted to see if I could take him away from that woman he married. What a perfect beauty. How I've always hated her. If I could take him from her, it'd mean I was more beautiful, wouldn't it?

"Well, Victoria," Journal says, "that's crazy."

Maybe. But I did it! I took him away from A. We traveled, we went to conferences, we did business deals, we shared five-star hotel suites. Always, he in his room, me in mine. No one knew. But, there's the truth of it.

What I don't understand is, why did he do it? Why did he ruin his marriage? I wanted to prove to myself that I could do it, and I did.

But I still don't understand why he let it happen.

Now, the problem is, I'm so bored. Always my problem. Always get bored. I wish he'd say, "This isn't working. I'm going back to A., if

And there, mid-sentence, the text quit. The rest of the little book was blank. That was the last entry. Alison sat in shock. Thinking to thumb through the pages in the front of the book, but no, really, not wanting to read any more.

She closed her eyes, trying to imagine Victoria writing these words, but she couldn't make the picture come to mind.

Finally she breathed heavily again and looked at Sage. "I don't know what ... what to say. I don't know what to think."

"I know. I know, Alison. Same for me. It has to be so much worse for you."

"Do you," Alison didn't want to ask the question, but she had to. "Do you think what she's written is the truth?"

"I do, Alison. Yes, I believe it's true, because of the part that involves me. Anthony did ... suggest we get married. It was too ... too weird. I mean, he's like my uncle. I just *couldn't* ... anyway, what she wrote is pretty much exactly what he said. That he was concerned about me and my future, and I'd always be taken care of. And he hoped it didn't seem too weird, because he knew it was. But, well, I said no, that was not an option, and he dropped the subject.

"And he has been sincerely happy about Michael and me. Sincerely. In fact, he's seemed sort of relieved that Michael and I are involved. Like he doesn't have to worry about me anymore."

Alison nodded. That all sounded like Anthony. But ... "Now what?" she said aloud.

"I cannot answer that question, Alison. Right or wrong, I'm only the messenger. You might do something, you might do nothing. Whatever you do, it's none of my business.

"But I will share with you, reading this part about how she put Anthony up to suggesting marrying me, playing on his soft heart, makes me feel ... I feel differently about her, and will never feel about her as I did before. Her pure, selfish greed is boggling. I refused to see it, though there it always was. But now that I have ...." She shook her head.

"I'm so sorry, Sage." Alison put her arm around her.

"I'm sorry too, Alison. What you've gone through!"

Alison shrugged. "I was an adult. But I don't think there's anything worse than using a young person to one's own ends."

"It *is* terrible," Sage agreed. "We can both feel sorry for one another and for ourselves. My goodness, how did she get to be such a terrible person, when my father was completely amazing. Completely kind, completely loving. How did they come from the same parents?"

"The world is fraught with that question, dear. You'll wear yourself out with it. Let us simply pity her, and move on with our lives."

"I will. Eventually. But I suspect I'll also often have bouts of anger."

"I can advise you not to. But I suspect it'll be the same for me."

They sat silently for a few moments, then Alison said, "I got an interesting message from Evin practically the same moment I got yours."

"Oh? Best wishes for your opening?"

"Yes. And more."

"Yes?"

"He said he'd had a dream. He said that he dreamt that I was head to head, talking with Thor. He said that he felt he understood the dream, and that he released me from his desire for us to be together."

"Oh, my. He desired for you to be together?"

"Yes. But—no more."

"What do you think? About his dream?"

"I suppose the most interesting aspect of his dream is that I had the exact same dream the same night he had his, maybe even at the same time, except I was head to head with Thor. And I woke with a start, wondering at the conversation between Thor and me. But I couldn't remember a word of it."

"Oh my, oh my. My, my, my, Alison. That's ... a ... amazing, I think it falls in the category of miracle."

"It seems so."

"So, Alison ...."

"Don't say anything right now, Sage. As Fate, or whatever it is, seems to be making a lot of moves, let's let it play out its hand."

"All right."

Alison closed the journal, turned the key in the

lock and put her hand over it, covering it. "Just the two of us know that these words were written. And I believe it remains for us to let it stay that way, unless and until something transpires that needs this clarification."

"That's fine, Allison," Sage nodded. "I'm in no rush to broadcast it. After all, it's still terribly new to me, too. I haven't sorted out my myriad thoughts and feelings. So a secret it remains. Unless clarification is needed."

Alison handed the journal to Sage. "Hide this away." She stood and stretched. "In the meantime, I must go through that gigantic pile of prints," she pointed to the corner of the room where stood a set of large sliding drawers,

"And see what I have that matches up with Mr. Styikes orders for my prints, then figure out what I must have made. See where each print is in the numbering sequence, and you know, all that artisty businessy stuff.

"Can I help?"

"You can be extremely helpful. I need you to do two things."

"Oh, goody. I'll do anything."

"Chore number one, I need you to keep Miss Prissy occupied as when I get out big prints, she thinks it's always for her particular play."

"Oh, that sounds really hard. Playing with a beautiful cat. I don't know if I can handle other assignments."

"I'll let you decide for yourself if you can handle both requests. The second one is to sit there with the cat and chat with me while you also chat with the cat."

Sage laughed, picking up Miss Prissy from the end of the sofa. "I'll do my best."

Chapter 16
Anthony

Alison spent the rest of the morning and the early afternoon with Sage, who did an excellent job of her two chores while she, herself got much done, organizing the prints.

In the afternoon she gathered all she'd organized and put them in a large art portfolio. "Time to go. I'm going to go as I am, and I'll drive my car. Poor thing, it rarely gets an outing. I trust you won't mind staying here continuing with your first chore."

"Not one bit," Sage affirmed. "I'll bet you've sold a ton more prints."

"Goodness, I hope not. It's a lot of work getting them together."

"But remember, what you love about being an artist is bringing happiness, peace, and joy into the lives of others."

"You listen too closely!"

"Not to everyone, but to you, yes." Sage grinned, snuggling Miss Prissy close.

Alison went down the rarely-used indoor back stairs, that, although they led to the street level, they seemed like basement stairs, dark and steep. She navigated them carefully carrying the oversized portfolio. At her car she placed the portfolio in the trunk, got into the car and pulled out of her garage. All without conscious thought. What occupied her mind was the remarkable movement of fate—or whatever it was. Destiny, serendipity, kismet ....

Victoria's confession in her journal ... could anyone in a million years have anticipated such a thing? And, as she reflected on those words, etched, now on her mind, replaying them, she had the insight that Victoria had only pursued Anthony because ... not because she wanted *him*. But because she hated his wife, her very own, sweet, kind, neighborly self. She had written that if she could steal Anthony away from his marriage, that would mean she was more beautiful than Alison.

What a ridiculous, and childish thought. People loved who they loved, with physical beauty not the deciding factor. A nice feature, perhaps, but not the deciding factor.

Of course, the most profound mystery revolved around Victoria's extremely pertinent question: Why *did* Anthony let Victoria destroy their marriage? Why? How did he let himself go from a loving relationship, with companionship, affection, and care for twenty years, to a completely loveless relationship?

"Well," she said aloud as she pulled up to Styikes Gallery, "no time to sort it out now. Destiny, it's in your hands."

She was sure she heard the universe chuckle. Yes. As if her fate was ever *not* in destiny's hands.

She jumped out and scurried to the open trunk, grateful that, although it was overcast, it was not raining. As she pulled the portfolio out, someone came behind her and took it from her hands.

She let out a small shriek as she turned, then saw Anthony. "Good lord, Anthony, give a girl some warning."

"Sorry. Let me carry this for you."

"Thank you. That would be helpful."

She felt strange and awkward with Anthony, and remained silent as they walked into the gallery. Mr. Styikes, talking with a customer, looked up and nodded to her. Jan was at the front desk. "Oh good, some more prints. I hope you brought some extras that are not on last night's list."

"Well, no I didn't. I do have a few that weren't on the list, but I didn't bring them. And then, there's a couple prints on the list I don't currently have. I have to get them printed and finessed with paint touches. And then, of course, they'll have to dry."

"Oh dear, Jan fretted. "Well, there are worse problems."

"Yes. Like not making any sales at all," Mr. Styikes said, coming up to them. "But that's not a problem with this show, that's for sure." He glanced at Anthony. "You'll excuse us as we sort out our business."

"Of course." Anthony nodded. "I'm here to continue taking in the Alison's work."

Alison and Mr. Styikes went into his office. She handed him the portfolio. He opened it and thumbed through the prints. "Excellent, Alison, truly. Some artists bring in prints that practically have to be completely retouched up, or are simply not acceptable. But yours are perfect."

"I keep them in blueprint file drawers."

"See? I'm forever telling artists to be professional and do like you do. It pays off in the end. You're going to have to produce quite a few prints as it is. I'm relieved that none of these are rejects. All right now, let's make a list of the prints you have, where you are in the print numbering of each, how many you have left in the print runs, and which have to be printed."

They were in Mr. Styikes office for over an hour, organizing the prints that were there, and sorting out how many, and which ones had to be made, and which ones she might make additional copies of for probable pending sales. Finally, they re-entered the gallery, Alison sighing a big sigh. "I'm so glad we have that all sorted out."

She looked around for Anthony, but didn't see him.

Jan caught her gaze. "Anthony went for a walk. He said he'd be right back. He said he felt he was getting on our nerves, but we said no, although, his pacing was kinda distracting."

"Oh, goodness, you should have been truthful. 'Yes, Anthony, your pacing is making us crazy and driving away customers.'"

"Oh, no," Jan said.

"That would not be truthful," Jen added.

"He made us laugh."

"Really!" Alison exclaimed. She'd never heard such a thing about Anthony before. If anything, he was too serious. And he didn't know how to tease.

"He said that, years ago, you told him that he neither knew how to take or give teasing."

"So he said he practiced giving it, and then he made us tease him."

"What did you tease him about?" Alison asked.

"Pacing up and down, like a caged tiger."

"But he said it was his way of meditating."

"And now he's gone for a meditative walk. At least that's what he said."

"Most interesting!" Alison felt a bit dizzy from looking back and forth from one to the other in their exchange. "And here he is now. Back from his Zen retreat," she said, facing the front window and seeing him approach the gallery.

"Zen retreat! *Funny!*" Both girls laughed.

"What's so funny?" he demanded as he came through the door.

"You. And your tiger pacing."

"You told," he chided.

"We did."

"Not nice."

'Very nice," Jan protested.

Anthony turned to Alison. "Are you nearly done?"

"I believe I'm completely done for today. And it's six o'clock, time to close up shop. I'm going to take my roses, I hope you don't mind," she said to Jan and Jen. "Gregory bought them for me, and, although they were wonderful in the gallery for the opening and first day, I rather selfishly, want to have them at home."

"Of course!" Jan and Jen chorused.

"I'll bring back the vase next week. Along with a bunch of prints."

"Okay. Oh!" Jan exclaimed. There's a little box in the back. Let me get it to put the flowers in."

"That would be perfect."

Alison waited for Jan's return in a rather strained, awkward silence.

Jan finally emerged from the back room, with a little box. "Sorry it took me so long. It got shoved behind some bigger boxes, and I couldn't find it."

Alison put the box on the counter and the flowers in the box, which fit perfectly. "Couldn't be a better! All right, then." She looked around for Mr. Styikes, saw him across the gallery with a customer. He caught her eye and she waved. He nodded and put a subtle thumb up in response, which amused her tremendously, as he was so formal—the casual gestures was incongruous and charming.

"All right then, she said again, looking at Jan and Jen. "I'll see you two in a few days."

"Yes, yes, they both grinned and nodded. "Great show, Alison. Congratulations."

"Could not have done it without the two of you!" She hurried through the door with her roses, with Anthony close behind.

He stowed the portfolio in the trunk, then took over the care of the roses.

Something entirely too ironic about the only man she had ever married carrying the roses of the man who had asked her to marry him less than twenty-four hours before. But she released that thought into the cosmos of her brain, to mull over at some other time.

She decided that this would be an excellent moment to remind herself that ....

She
> *Always*
>> *Landed*
>>> *On*
>>>> *Her*
>>>>> *Feet*

She pulled out of the parking space, her mantra banging up against her nerves. Here she was, for the first time in *years*, alone with Anthony.

"At last," he said quietly. "Alone together."

"Yes." She said. "I ... I don't know where to go, I don't know what to do."

"How about going to where the land ends, and we listen to the ocean lap to shore."

"All right." She drove from downtown, across town, through Golden Gate Park, out through the avenues, and finally, to the ocean. It was night, and the sky was overcast. There was nothing to see, but they could hear the swish-splash-swish of the ocean hugging the sand.

Alison found a place to park and turned off the engine. They sat in silence while moments ticked by. She began to wonder if Anthony was having second thoughts—a myriad second thoughts —about what he intended to say.

Finally he said, "Would it surprise you if I told you I have never, ever, stopped loving you?"

"*Ahm*, no. It maybe would have in the past. But at this juncture, no. I ... I believe you."

"I suspect, though, that there are some other things I could tell you that would surprise you."

Alison thought, well, yes. As short a while ago as this morning, that would have been true. "Such as?" she dared to say aloud.

"Such as ..." he paused, and seemed to struggle with what he would say, and how he would say it, struggling with the box in his hands, and the roses nearly in his face.

Alison took the box and set it in the back seat. "Let's not forget them."

"Of course not. Damn other men, anyway. No, I don't mean that. You are an amazing, beautiful, woman, and you attract amazing men. Present company excepted."

"No, Anthony," she said, screwing up her bravery. "Present company not excepted."

"Really? You don't think I'm a heel, a cad, a miscreant?"

"A reprobate, a scoundrel, a louse?" she continued. "My goodness, let's practice name calling."

Anthony chuckled a wry chuckle.

"No. None of those honorifics seem appropriate for you. Lacking in strength at times, yes. Succumbing to a weakness, yes."

"Yes, Alison, I will neither disagree nor try to change your mind. I think you've exceptionally clearly defined—me. I am weak, in the most unpleasant way, at times. Or have been. But I decided to change that. To shift my self-belief, and to change my self-image. I can be strong, although perhaps a bit graceless, as this aspect of strength is new to me.

"Like last night, forcing my presence on your opening. I've berated myself for almost twenty-four hours now for that selfishness. But I'm trying to be stronger while still sensitive. Do you know that's a fairly tough assignment? Especially for a man, whom society has socialized in an unbalanced fashion. If you're strong then your not sensitive. If you're sensitive, then you're weak. To find the balance between the two...."

"Yes. I can see it's not easy. But are we going to talk in abstracts, or are we going to get concrete?"

"Abstracts are less dangerous, but get nowhere. And concrete could, perhaps, bring our lovely ocean side chat to an abrupt end."

"No abrupt end, Anthony. I agreed to talk with you, and I'm going to stand by my promise. But, candidly, I do wish you'd speak your mind."

"All right then. Way back when, when things started to go awry between us, because of, well, you know who. I couldn't believe it was happening. I couldn't even observe myself and understand what I was doing. What did I think? I still can't put myself in my own mind, back then."

"Perhaps that was because you were out of your own mind," Alison offered.

"Well, yes. Maybe you tease, but I think you're absolutely correct. Somehow, I got crazy. I even saw I'd become crazy, but I couldn't stop. So strange. I was like two people but the smart one was outside of the container of 'me.'

"But even in all the madness, I never, *not for a moment*, stopped loving you. How she came between us, I still don't quite get. It was like a kind of magic, some sort of spell. I wanted to be with you, but I went traipsing off with her. Hither and thither. To conventions, to horse shows, to whatever. And I never ... I never ... I always ...."

"You never and always, what?"

"I always wished you were there. I can *not* explain to you how weird it was. And I know I sound like any other man caught in the wrong, the very, *very* wrong, and I would dare to try to say I never did wrong. But, of course, it was all wrong. Wrong, wrong, wrong."

"So why do you say you might try to dare to say you did *not* do wrong?"

"Because. Because of something you won't believe."

"Try me."

"Because she and I ... she wasn't, and I didn't ... because of you ... we, I know you won't believe me, but it never happened between us. I know you won't believe me."

"But if what you say is true, then ... why were you with her? Why did you appear to have stopped loving me?"

"I never stopped loving you. But I messed up unforgivably because, and I don't even know how to apologize for this, but at that time, and, again, I've completely changed about this ...."

Please do go on, Anthony. Or rather do *NOT* go on, but make your point."

"All right. Here it is. The terrible child I was. I felt like you left me for your art. You were getting so into your art and going to this art show, and taking that art class, and meeting this artist and that artist. You had a whole slew of new friends, and you had this shocking talent that came roaring to the surface.

"You'd talked about doing art. And that was all fine and good. And you started dabbling, and that was fine and good, as well. But then you started to get noticed, and you were painting and sketching and thinking art and talking art. And I didn't know anything about your contemporary art world. I know classic stuff. But I didn't know or understand your world. You'd say something by so-and-so was remarkable. I couldn't see it. I had no eye for it.

He paused, looking out at the eternally arriving and leaving tide. He sighed deeply and continued. "And it felt like you had grown away from me. I had this deep, deep feeling that you were going to leave me. Which you did. But I mean, even before you did, you ... you left me. And I was a spoiled little boy. I wanted you to hurt like I was hurting. There's not excuse for it. I'm simply telling you my truth of that time.

"I was a spoiled little boy, I was threatened and probably jealous of you developing yourself, jealous of your self-awareness, of your self-growth. What I did was unforgivable, while what you did was evolved and beautiful.

"There are times when I think that men really are inferior. Sometimes our reasoning is ... not reasonable. Well, there are some men who are even-keeled, and evolved. Like these two running the race to Alison. Evin and Gregory. Who will win?"

Alison ignored that comment. "What do you feel about my art now?" Now, this was the most important question. What *did* he think of her art?—She'd never heard before what he'd just said. She would not have even been able to imagine it.

"I *love* your art, Alison. Now I've gazed at your magnificent talent and have gotten your message."

"My message?"

"Yes. To be in the moment. To drink in every moment, no matter how small it may seem. Because in every moment, *there are all moments*. Because time is like a fractal, repeating forms. The tiniest is the greatest.

"Ever since you left, I'm haunted by the small moments. The littlest thing can trigger an entire series of thoughts. Thoughts of you riding on Twinkle's mother, you, laughing with Clara, you graciously entertaining guests. The mansion is haunted by you. My life is haunted by you. And, I guess I've destroyed any hope of a future with you. But I had to tell you this. And tell you some things that I know you won't believe, but I have to say them, because, well, because I have to."

"Besides the one thing I've told you that didn't happen, about which, I note, you've said nothing one way or another, here's another completely unpleasant thing. I mean, it seems like it, but that was not my intention. Wildly as far from that as one could get."

"Concrete, please."

"She who shall not be named, got it in her rather twisted mind that I ought ... I choke to even say this, but I must say it. That I ought to marry Sage. Now, don't freak out. But, the idea was that she would be protected for life with the security of my finances.

"It seemed quite logical the way it was put to me, and so I suggested it to Sage. She was grace personified, although I saw immediately that the idea shocked her. Shocked her and rocked her. I tried to backpedal, to soften it. But, and as I saw, she was so gracious, but I really knocked her for a loop with my suggestion.

"Still, the idea haunted me. Especially after ... after that shocking death, I thought, all right, it's true, men are going to be preying on Sage. And she's so young and she will make inexperienced choices. And if I was in the position to legally keep her holdings and finances safe, then, well, she'd be safe. It was a crazy idea.

"I can't tell you, Alison, no one is happier than I am that she and Michael have finally discovered each other. So obvious from the outset, but, what can you do when people can't even see what's in front of them?"

"Yes, Anthony. I'm feeling rather that way myself."

"What ... what are you saying?"

"I'm saying, for the last two nights I've had dreams about Thor. Then I got a message from Evin yesterday that he had the same dream as I did, that I was head to head, talking with Thor."

"That can't be good, Evin having the same dream as you."

"Not good for Evin, that's true. He wrote that he realized that he had to remove himself from any notion of a relationship with me. I didn't know what to think of the two of us having the same dream. Then a series of events happened, but, to top it all off, you came to my opening ...."

"Which you pointed out to me was completely selfish of me, and disruptive for you."

"True, I did say that. But, you were right when you said I'd kept you at arm's reach, mostly because of something I'd overheard at your birthday party, which now, both you and Sage have clarified. However, last weekend, although I had a truly wonderful time, I wanted to get back home and put my mind to getting

my show up. But then, that freesia bridge, with you
standing at it, like you were trying to make a decision,
and I ... I was so confused. I didn't want to be confused.
I had to take care of my responsibilities.

"Add to all of that, last night, what you had to
say about *Freesia Bridge*, how it came right from your
childhood, how, even months ago, I started that painting
with no clue where it came from. With that, and the Thor
dreams, and ...."

"I'm so glad you put the flowers in the back seat,"
Anthony interrupted.

"The flowers in the back seat? What does that have
to do with why you?...."

"It makes it so much easier to..." He put his arms
around her and kissed her cheek, "get closer ..." He kissed
her neck. "and closer." He kissed her on the mouth.

"How can I tell you how much I've missed you?"
He whispered.

"You're doing excellently," Alison answered.

She let the years, the confusion, the loneliness,
the effort to close her heart against him—all, *all fall
away*.

And she could no longer—nor did she need
to!—resist his kisses, which she began to return. How
wonderful he felt, how gorgeous he looked in the
faint, faint, moonlight that peeked out through the
clouds.

This, *this* was the feeling she feared, was it only last
night? Ah, that insight she had last night, that she could
only feel *this way* about *This. Very. Man.*

"Can you love me again, my precious, darling Ali-
girl? Can we make it work?"

"I can't love you again, since, with all the hurt and anger I've felt toward you—and it's been considerable, I never stopped loving you. One thing I learned is that it *is* possible to love and hate someone at the same time. Though I much prefer to not be so conflicted."

"Oh Alison, what I did to you! Your ocean of forgiveness is bigger than the Pacific." He looked out at the ocean. "Thank you, thank you, all the *Powers that Be*. Thank you for giving me another chance to honor this perfect love.

"We're going to have challenges, because you've made a full and wonderful life for yourself here, and I have no expectations—*no desire!*—that you compromise it. But, if I know you love me, that's all that matters. I will love you in the spaces apart, as well as when we're together. I'm ... I've grown up. A little, at least. I no longer feel competitive with your creations. I'm so proud of you."

"I am glad to hear it. I have my art classes, and my students. Oh, there's a lot to think about but, yes, as long as I love and am loved, I can do anything."

"Yes." Anthony hesitated.

"What?"

"*Hmmm,* in the spirit of full disclosure, there is one more thing I must confess."

Oh no, Alison thought, the monster under the bed. Or perhaps *in* the bed ... "Please don't tell me something I can't endure."

"I sincerely hope it's not something you can't endure. But, *hmmm,* you need to know that we needn't get married again."

"*Ahm*," Alison felt confused. "Are we ready to talk about marriage?"

"Probably not. But, what I'm hemming and hawing about is that, I, *ahh*, never filed the divorce papers. And so, rather technically, we're not exactly divorced."

"Oh, wait, no. Oh, that's strange. So strange. But what if I'd gotten married again?"

"I'm happy to confess that I'm delighted you haven't. But if you had, you would have been all right because you hired an attorney and filled out all the proper paperwork."

"And I got the settlement."

"Well, of course, Alison. I would have given you that settlement under any circumstance. I directed my attorney to give you whatever you asked for."

"Which was not my asking, but my attorney's communication with your attorney. I was a bit stunned when I saw what my attorney had managed to settle on."

"He didn't ask for enough. After I attended to his requests, I had my attorney append to it. He thought I was insane. He said he'd never seen such a thing."

"So, should I be upset with you for not divorcing me?"

"Please don't be. And thank you for believing my rather unbelievable confession."

"When I contemplate the chain of events that has clicked into place over the last few days, to find myself here with you, like this, talking of love and the future, I can only shrug and set aside any resistance. In the end, I believe in love."

"Of course, you believe in love, and I believe in love. And in the new beginning."

"Yes. And in the new beginning," Alison agreed, kissing her *husband* again. And yet again.

The End

Would you like a free copy of **Canyon Road,** *Book One* in the **Canyon Road Love Stories** series? I'll happily send it to you an ebook edition exchange for a review.

Write to me with your request:

Thea@EmersonandTilman.com

About The Author….

I'm a full-time writer, creating the worlds in my novels, in the Portland, Oregon area. Having lived in a variety of locations around the world, I happily settled in the beautiful Northwest, where the environment and culture are perfect for a writing life. The rain, the forests, the water falls, mountains, and ocean—plus lots of writers—make it a great place to be a writer.

Thank you beforehand if you're inspired to write a kind review–which is warmly received. If you have questions or comments, or would like to know about new releases of my books, write to me – I'd love to hear from you!

Thea@emersonandtilman.com

www.ingramcontent.com/pod-product-compliance
Lightning Source LLC
Chambersburg PA
CBHW071301190726
48292CB00007B/2642